SECRET CHARM

JILL SANDERS

GRAYTON

DIGITAL ISBN: 978-1-945100-41-3

PRINT ISBN: 9798417317293

Print ISBN: 978-1-945100-71-0

Copyeditor: Erica Ellis – inkdeepediting.com

To my kids.

SUMMARY

You'd think that being forced to move to paradise would be, well, heaven. But for Nicky, it means the end of her career and her lifelong dream of becoming an investigative journalist. After all, nothing exciting ever happens on a small island. The only perk to the job is having to work side by side with her new scuba instructor, the charming and extremely hunky Beau.

Beau has only ever wanted to be in one place his entire life. The Hawaiian Islands are the most beautiful place on Earth, and trust him, he's been to enough places to make that determination. When he's hired to train and oversee Nicky's crew, he thinks it's just another job. But then the bullets start flying and the training that he gained in his years in Special Forces are the only thing that can save the pair of them. That and his knowledge of his beautiful home.

PROLOGUE

Beau Montgomery lay in the sand and looked up at the sky as his breathing calmed and his hearing returned. Small perfectly puffy clouds floated overhead, making him believe, if just for a second, that everything was calm. Just another day on the large blue rock.

Then bits of sand and rock flew by his head as another blast sounded not far from his hiding spot. He knew he had to move. His life depended on it. But for a few precious heartbeats, his body refused to obey his mind.

The sound of another blast had him jerking free of the trance and rolling over. He crab-crawled for as long as he could, his heavy pack and gun slowing his flight.

There was nothing more he could do back there. He'd seen the explosion that had taken out three members of his team. Had watched their body parts fly through the air. There hadn't even been time for them to scream. Just... death.

He knew the Beta team was a few clicks behind the Alpha team, which he'd been a member of for the past two years.

He pushed the names and faces of his three comrades, his three friends, to the back of his mind. What he needed to focus on now was getting away and warning the rest of the teams.

They'd been lied to by their informant. This route was still controlled by the enemy.

It felt like he'd been crawling for hours. His elbows and knees ached with each push forward. When the sounds of flying bullets started fading, he glanced around and figured that he could either chance it by standing up and running for his life or he could lie there in the sand and join the rest of his team.

He jumped up and sprinted as fast as he could. He thought about dropping his pack, of leaving all of the essentials he'd carted through the desert, but he thought better of it when he realized he'd need those supplies to survive.

He'd lost so much in a single day and, as he ran, he wondered how he was ever going to recover.

This hadn't even been his team's scariest mission. They'd been on radio silence since the moment they left base two days ago. The Beta team would be a full day behind them and he had to let them know they were walking into a trap.

Suddenly, his lifelong dream surfaced. He hadn't thought about it in a while and a calm peace came over him the more he thought about it.

As he ran for his life over the next day and a half, he promised himself with each step that if he made it out of the desert alive, he would follow his heart.

CHAPTER ONE

T wo years later...

Beau lay in the sand. This time, the sound of waves crashing a few feet away from him soothed his soul. He carried scars on the inside from that day long ago, but outside, he appeared as calm as the wind on that perfect Hawaiian day.

"Aloha, Beau," someone called to him.

He didn't even lift his head to see who it was. Instead, he just waved his hand and called out, "Aloha."

When he'd returned home after his retirement, he'd followed his heart, which had led him to the most beautiful place on Earth. The Hawaiian Islands.

He'd found his home through an old friend, whose parents had handed the place down to him after their death. He'd gotten the deal of a lifetime since Mateo had been stationed in Europe and had no desire to return to his childhood home.

Beau had spent the first year remodeling the four-bedroom place and had even built a swimming pool with his own hands. Basically, in the past two years he'd done anything and everything he could to forget that day. He'd buried his brothers and sister in arms and carried the guilt and shame of being the only survivor from Alpha team.

"There you are," someone said directly overhead, blocking out the sun.

Squinting, he looked up and held in a groan. Kailani stood looking down at him, her hands on her hips. He couldn't see the look on her face, since the sun was behind her, but most likely it was a disapproving look.

"I have been looking for you," Kailani said firmly. "You have a job."

"Today?" he groaned, knowing he sounded like a child, but he had spent the last five days rebuilding the patio off the back of his house and every muscle on his body was aching. He'd hoped for a day off lying on the beach in the sun.

After his first year on the island, he'd been asked to help out Mateo's family's business. Kailani was Mateo's younger sister. She and her extended family ran a popular snorkeling, scuba, and excursion business near the best resort on the island.

Which meant they had a lot of business. All of the time. Kailani had pretty much blackmailed him to helping them out a few days a week. Plus, she'd hinted that he had a bunch of free time and that there would be extra spending cash to help with the remodel. Plus, there'd be a steady stream of women hanging on him. The cash he needed, the women, not so much.

At first, he'd been thankful for the distraction and the extra cash, which had indeed helped fund his remodeling.

He also liked interacting with the tourists... some of the time.

Today was not going to be one of those days.

"I've got a big spender. A group that needs some special attention for a job that might last a couple weeks. A couple of them need some scuba instruction, but for the most part, it's just taking them out each day and babysitting. You interested?" Kailani asked, motioning to a group of four people standing near the small hut that was the business's main office.

He was about to make some excuse as to why he didn't have the next couple weeks free, but then he spotted the pretty sandy-blonde woman leaning against the hut, watching them. He didn't know what was more impressive, the fact that she looked bored while standing on the beach, or the fact that she was actually wearing heeled sandals in the sand.

But the instant spark of lust he felt for the blonde had him realizing just how long it had been since he'd felt anything close to attraction.

"Are you interested or not? Cuz, if not I could get—"

"No." He sat up and then ran his hands through his dark unruly hair, shaking the sand from it. He'd let it grow long on top, which meant it was falling in his eyes all the time now. "I've got this."

Kailani smiled and wiggled her eyebrows. "I figured as much." She nodded towards the blonde and then turned and started walking back to the hut. "She's a journalist. She'll see right through your bullshit," she threw over her shoulder with a chuckle.

He chuckled. Kailani had grown to be like a sister to him. He'd known her since she was five, when Beau and his family had moved to Hawaii after his father had been stationed in Honolulu. Less than a year later, his father had been killed during a shooting on the military base. Some twenty-year-old kid with a semi-automatic had taken his father's life and those of six others that day.

Beau and his mother had lived on the island until he was sixteen, when his mother had met and married Carl, a rancher on vacation, and moved back to Wyoming with him. Two years later, Beau had joined the Forces and left the negative-degree weather behind forever.

Dusting the sand off his board shorts, he followed Kailani back across the beach to the rental hut. He noticed the blonde's eyes following him as he approached and tried desperately not to trip in the sand and land on his face. After all, it been several years since he'd tried to do anything that resembled flirting.

"Aloha. Morning," he added, stopping by the woman. "Kailani tells me you need a boat and some scuba guidance?"

A thin, balding man in long dress pants and a short-sleeved button-up shirt stepped forward and held out his hand. "I'm Jake Drammen, this is Leo." He motioned to a heavy-set older white guy in khaki shorts and a button-up shirt, holding several large black bags. "This is Gordy." He motioned to a younger black man in board shorts and a tank top, whose attention was fully on a group of young women playing volleyball on the beach. "And this is—"

"Nicole Cardone," the blonde said, stepping forward and giving her colleague a side look. She was wearing a white wraparound skirt and a soft blue button-up shirt. He could see a bright blue swimsuit underneath the outfit. Her long blonde hair was braided and lying on her shoulder. Her face was clear of product, and he imagined wouldn't need any. Her natural beauty was almost blinding.

Nicole? The name was a little too formal for someone like her. He wondered instantly if she went by Nicky.

"I'm Beau. It appears I'll be showing you the ropes and taking you out on the water," he said easily. "Have you got all your gear settled?" He motioned to the scuba gear.

Jake stepped forward. "I hope you're a professional. As I was telling Kallina here..."

"Kailani," Beau corrected, even though Kailani was busy and helping a couple from the resort who were renting snorkel equipment.

"Kailani," Jake corrected impatiently. "My crew will be filming offshore for the next few days, possibly longer."

"Right." He nodded. "Are any of you certified?" he asked the crew.

Two of them, including Nicole, raised their hands. Gordy shrugged. "I got through two lessons."

"This is my most experienced team. It's why I chose them," Jake said, sounding even more annoyed.

"Right." He motioned towards the docks across the sand. "After an hour of basic instructions, maybe a little more for Gordy, I'll have you three in the water and on your way."

"Keep me posted," Jake said to Nicole. "I'll see you back at the hotel later."

"Right," Nicole said with a nod before bending over and helping with the heavy scuba equipment that Kailani had already set them up with. He had his own on his boat already, along with extra oxygen tanks and other standard gear.

Beau stooped and easily picked up a box to help.

"Your boat?" Leo asked. "I hope she's big enough."

"For the four of us?" he asked. "No doubt."

"How long have you been doing this?" Leo asked.

The older man looked a little red and was already breathless, and they hadn't even made it halfway across the sand.

"This?" he asked, stopping, and taking the man's heavy bag from him so that he didn't strain himself.

"Thanks," Leo said. He continued to follow him towards the docks.

"I've been scuba diving since I was nine. I've been taking others out for the past year," he answered.

"Only a year?" Leo asked, trying to keep up with him.

"How many dives in Hawaii have you been on?" he asked the man since it was obvious that he needed to put the man at ease.

"Two," he answered.

"How about the rest of you?" He threw the question to Nicole and Gordy.

"Never," Gordy answered quickly.

"Around a dozen," Nicole answered, sounding bored. "It's why Jake picked me instead of..." She stopped and took a deep breath, then shook her head.

"Have somewhere else to be?" he asked Nicole.

"Not Hawaii," she said under her breath.

"Kailani didn't mention where we were heading," he said, giving Nicole all of his attention. He'd assumed that the crew would be heading to Shipwreck Beach like most of the tourists he took out on the water.

"We'll be going about thirty miles west," Nicole answered.

Beau's eyebrows shot up. "What's thirty miles out?" he asked, already knowing but asking anyway as they stepped onto the dock.

"Something, I hope," she answered under her breath.

He stopped at the *Ho'omau* and set the box and bag

down. "This is us." He motioned to his boat. It had taken over a month for him to sand and repaint the hull himself.

"Nice," Gordy said, jumping on board and looking around the powder-blue double-decker Viking 77.

"This is all ours for the duration?" Leo asked as he stepped on board.

"She's mine, but I'll let you ride in her," he joked as he helped Nicole cross onto the deck.

She took his hand and started to step over the gap but stopped.

"What does…"—she glanced down at the bold black letters he'd painted on the back— "*Ho'omau*, mean?"

"Steady as you go," he answered with a smile.

She seemed to think about it for a moment, then nodded and passed over the gap.

"You can store the scuba gear in the bins there." He motioned to the long white storage areas along the back of the boat. "We'll put your camera gear inside out of the weather," he told Leo before he gathered the rest of the stuff and stepped on board himself.

"In here," he told Leo and Gordy, who followed him across the main deck on the back of the boat. After all of their scuba gear was stored, all three of them followed him up the few steps into the main cabin area.

His boat wasn't the nicest or biggest around the islands, but it was close. He'd decided to splurge, since he planned on spending a lot of time on it. And, besides that, it had already paid for itself with charters he'd earned over the past year.

Stepping into the main cabin, he took the left stairs to below deck.

"You can store your equipment in one of the quarters." He ducked at the base of the stairs and opened the door to one of the two crew quarters. Each one had two bunkbeds and shared a bathroom across the narrow hall.

"Wow," Gordy gasped as he stepped past Beau. "Why don't we just stay here instead of that stuffy resort?"

Leo grunted in response. Gordy turned as the heavier man was struggling to get down the narrow staircase.

"Right," Gordy said. "Sorry, Leo. I forgot you don't like being on the water."

"You don't?" Beau asked, concerned. "You don't get seasick, do you?"

"No, just... I'm claustrophobic," Leo answered.

"Oh. Then go ahead and head back upstairs. We'll store all this." He took the bag from Leo's hands and then motioned towards the stairs.

When they were alone, Gordy shook his head. "I'm not sure why the boss wanted Leo on this assignment. The dude is a week away from a heart attack. I don't know how he's going to..." The man shut his mouth suddenly and shook his head. "There were younger cameramen."

"Well, there's no substitute for experience," he said, setting down the last bag. "All this is cameras?"

"Cameras and other equipment we'll need."

Since the man was in a talkative mood, he figured he'd get a little more info out of him.

"What does Nicole do?" he asked.

"Nicky? She's the journalist. The one we put in front of those." He shook his head. "A damn good one too. I've only worked with her a few times, but damn... the girl is good."

So she did go by Nicky, Beau thought with a smile as the man continued to talk.

"I'm not sure why they decided to move her here though. She had a promising career in San Fran." He shook his head.

"She lives here?" he asked, interested.

Gordy shrugged. "Until they decide to relocate her again."

"What is it you three are actually filming thirty miles out?" he asked after he realized the man had been avoiding the topic.

"Um." Gordy's eyes moved to the door. "We'd better head out, don't you think? Losing daylight and all."

"Right." He started up the stairs and found Leo and Nicky talking in the main cabin area.

"This is certainly more than we'd expected," Nicky said, motioning to the cabin.

"We aim to please," he said casually. "So, before we embark, there are a few safety features that we need to talk about." While he ran through where all the life vests and fire extinguishers were located on the boat, he watched Nicky closely and wondered if she felt the same pull of attraction that he did.

CHAPTER TWO

What the hell was she doing in Hawaii? She had been a few heartbeats away from a promotion to top investigative journalist at Shock Wave Editorials back in San Francisco, a position she'd been vying for since moving there almost three years ago.

Plus, she was supposed to be halfway around the world at her cousin Isabella's wedding tomorrow in Venice.

Instead, Jake had convinced everyone that she should be assigned to Maui for the next few months so she could take lead on this story. She liked the lead part, but the story? Not so much. Jake claimed it would be the story of the century, but he'd barely divulged any details to her yet. He'd said he would give her more details after meeting his informant and before he headed back to the mainland.

For the next four weeks, she was going to be stuck on a boat off the coast of Maui. And for what? A hint of a story that may or may not be true? She doubted that Jake knew what was going on himself. From what she had researched herself, there was no evidence of any conspiracy or even a threat of one. This story was a waste.

She still didn't understand why Jake had chosen her for this project. Her only working theory was that he was trying to keep her from getting the lead position back home. That's what she'd been thinking the entire trip across the ocean. Then she'd stepped into the dining room of the hotel late the previous night and had caught Jake and a very busty blonde making out in the bar.

She'd never been so angry. Her boss had dragged her across the ocean so that he could sit in an upscale resort and have an affair on the company's dime.

Then, during their breakfast meeting, he'd told them that he wouldn't be joining them out on the water that day. He claimed that he'd eaten something off and wasn't feeling well, but she knew. She'd seen the blonde woman standing around the outdoor tiki bar, looking bored and glancing their way several times.

After the three of them had finished getting fitted for both snorkeling and scuba gear, which they would be using for the duration, she'd watched Kailani walk across the sand and get their tour guide.

Just seeing the sexy, shirtless hunk lying in the sand had her heartrate spiking. Her only defense when his rich brown eyes had landed on her across the sand was to look bored.

He moved like an islander, as if there was no power on earth that could make him hurry. He was either dark complected or extremely tan.

She'd tried to maintain the bored look all through his introductions. She'd succeeded with her ruse up until Beau had taken her hand and helped her step onto the boat. When his hand had taken hers, she'd about lost her cool. She'd said the first thing that had come into her mind and asked what the name of the boat meant.

Steady as you go. Yeah, that described the man to a tee. He was steady. Rock solid and full of yummy muscles that she'd like to play with.

He remained shirtless, which meant she had plenty of time to admire all the toned muscles that ran across his arms and chest and down over his stomach and hips. God, that little spot just above his hips that dipped... She shook her head clear.

She tried very hard to avoid looking at his stomach area so she wouldn't get caught gawking, but hell, he was too delicious.

While he showed her and Gordy around the boat and talked about all the safety measures, she tried to focus on what he was saying. Really, she did.

The boat was gorgeous. She'd never been on a yacht before, but this was what she'd imagined it would look like. It was probably smaller than a full-blown yacht, but not by much.

Below deck, there were two full-sized bedrooms, by boat standards, and two smaller ones that held two bunkbeds each. There were three bathrooms and a half bath up on the main level, which Leo was grateful for since he claimed he was claustrophobic and didn't want to go down the stairs again.

She'd only worked with Leo a few times before and had worked with Gordy even less. She would have preferred her regular camerawoman, Kathia, and her normal sound engineer, Steven. Kat knew just how to get Nicky in the right light, and she worked great with Steven. But Leo's reputation preceded him at the network, and he was Jake's right-hand man for some reason.

Still, she wondered why this crew? Leo was seriously overweight, and Gordy was inexperienced with diving. She knew that both Kat and Steven were scuba certified since she'd gone on another job with them late last year.

"So, were to?" Beau asked, breaking into her thoughts.

She had the directions on her phone. Jake had sent them to her earlier that morning during their meeting. He'd also told her that it was imperative that their mission remain secret. He didn't want all the locals spreading the word about what they were doing and where they were diving.

Their informant had stressed to Jake that if the wrong people knew what they were looking into, there could be trouble.

What kind of trouble could someone get into on a small island anyway? It was Hawaii, not the Middle East, a place Nicky had been to twice in the past three years.

"Just head west," she answered, following Beau up a narrow set of stairs. Her eyes bored into his backside. The board shorts didn't cling to him but were tight enough that her imagination could fill in the rest.

At least she'd have something nice to look at while she chased a stupid dead end that Jake had probably made up in the first place so that he could get her out of the way and get a paid vacation with his lover. At least she'd have a nice tan by the time she went home.

Her bad mood was spreading as she followed Beau up the narrow stairs to what she assumed was the topmost level of the massive boat. At least she wouldn't be stuck in a small fishing boat like the last time she'd been on assignment on the water.

She'd been researching the disappearance of a family on a private yacht off the coast of Florida. The tragic ending hadn't been the one everyone was hoping for, but at least the husband, who had faked his own death after killing his young wife, was now rotting in a cell thanks to her. Their young son, whom he'd kidnapped, was now safe with the wife's sister.

This trip was nothing like that one. The more she thought about the treasure hunt, the more she realized she should have submitted her resume to a few more companies last month when she'd thought about switching jobs. But, as with most things she did, she'd waffled and ended up on a wild goose chase.

"So, princess." Beau smiled at her. She knew he was trying to flirt, but she was in no way a princess.

"Nope," she said, shaking her head.

"Yeah." He chuckled. "It sounded wrong the moment it left my lips. You're more of a koa." He nodded. "Warrior," he translated for her.

She nodded, liking the sound of it much more. She was a warrior. She needed to be. "Sure, whatever," she said with a shrug.

"It would be helpful to have more information than just 'head west'" he said, motioning to one of the three black leather chairs that sat next to the captain's chair. She took the seat next to his as he started the boat.

"For now, just head out." She watched as he picked up a walkie talkie and coordinated their departure with a dock hand, who untied them from the docks. "Why such a big boat?" she asked as they made their way slowly out of the port.

He glanced over at her. "Most tourists want to take long fishing trips or cruise around the islands and spend a few nights letting the waves rock them to sleep." He shrugged. "I wouldn't think you'd complain."

"I'm not, it's just..." She shrugged. "It seems a little overkill for a scuba and snorkeling guide."

"It is." He chuckled. "It's my private vessel. Kailani asked me to lend a hand, and the *Ho'omau* came with me."

"Are you a native?" she asked, curious.

"My mother is half Hawaiian. She's in Wyoming now," he answered, and she felt herself shiver as she remembered the one and only time she'd gone to the state. She'd been reporting on a huge blizzard that had killed more than half a dozen people, thanks to the power grid not being up to speed. The power company hadn't been too pleased by what she'd found out. Because of her reporting, those families had gotten answers.

"Too cold," she said, under her breath.

He laughed, and the rich deep sound made her smile.

"I completely agree. Where are you from?" he asked her easily.

"Originally? Colorado. Lately, San Francisco, where it's warmer. Not as warm as here, but I don't have to shovel snow from my driveway. You?"

"I grew up on the islands and moved to Wyoming with my mother during my teen years. I left as quickly as I could," he added as they started traveling faster. "West?" he asked, motioning to the computer screen. She wondered why the quick change of subject.

"West." She nodded in agreement.

He glanced over at her, and his eyes narrowed. "You don't seem like the type."

"What type?" she asked.

"Mea imi waiwai. Treasure hunter." He turned towards her a little more as his eyes ran over her. "Your boss mentioned this was for a story. The only reason anyone around here wants to go west is to look for Lokelani's treasure."

"Oh?" She knew how to play it cool. After all, she'd

bluffed her way through too many interviews to count. "What's that?"

His brown eyes narrowed as they ran over her slowly. She felt her entire body heat under his gaze.

"Something tells me that you already know. The question is why are a journalist and her camera crew treasure hunting?" He turned back to the front, and it was her turn to run her eyes over him.

"I'm just following orders," she finally admitted.

"Going to let me in on the scoop?" He nudged her knee with his own. "After all, you've got my undivided attention for the next few weeks."

She held in a groan. "Don't remind me."

He smiled and her breath caught at how sexy and perfect his smile was. "Rather be somewhere else?"

Figuring that it wouldn't hurt to tell the truth, she nodded. "Italy, to be exact. My cousin is getting married tomorrow."

"In Italy?"

"Venice. We have a very large extended family over there."

"Venice is nice."

"You've been?" she asked.

"A few times." He leaned back in the chair. "What does Nicky do outside of work?" he asked her.

She chuckled. "Not much." She motioned around them. "What does Beau do?"

"This is it. Oh, and I've been rebuilding my home for the past two years." He shrugged.

"Two years? Money issues or just laziness?"

He laughed. "I like that you're right up front."

"You don't get to be a good investigative journalist by beating around the bush."

"Right," he agreed. "It's pure laziness on my part. I'll work my ass off for a few weeks, then want time to recover as I figure out the next phase. Oh, and then there's the supply issues. I waited over three months for my new windows." He shook his head. "Which was not fun, since I had large gaping holes in my walls during the rainy season."

"When is the rainy season in Hawaii?" she asked, causing him to laugh.

"Every day around noon," he answered. She smiled.

"Okay, so you know boats, fishing, scuba diving, and construction..." She tilted her head and waited.

"If you're asking me what else there is to me..." He shrugged as a dark looked crossed those sexy brown eyes. "Not much."

She knew instantly that was a lie. She'd seen darkness in eyes like that before, and she realized he was suppressing a great sadness.

"Ex-military?" she asked on a whim.

He looked slightly surprised, but then nodded and changed the subject again. "You're a straight-shooting journalist who likes warm places, and whose family is more important than treasure hunting." His smile was back.

"That's about it." She smiled. "I've been known to curl up to with good mystery, oh, and I love chocolate."

He laughed. "I think both of those are on my list as well."

"Why come back to Hawaii? I mean, it sounds like you've traveled a little..." The dark look was back in his eyes, and he even glanced away from her. "So why come back here?"

"Why the Lokelani treasure?" he countered. "The last I heard; most treasure hunters had given up on finding the boat. It did go down in the eighteen twenties, after all. From what I've heard, it traveled from Peru to Lanai loaded full of treasure, payment in full for the hand of Peru's princess."

"Five hundred million dollars' worth of treasure today, roughly," she replied with a shrug. "I've done my research."

"Right." He smiled. "So, why?"

The look in his eyes released the lock that was normally placed firmly over her lips.

"Because my boss..." She rolled her eyes when she thought of Jake. The man was an idiot. Not only had she butt heads with the slimeball in the past three years, but he'd put her on some shitty assignments after she turned down his advances. "Jake decided that I was the only journalist who could cover the story. Which means I'm reassigned here until I get the scoop. Besides, he's an idiot who is cheating on his wife with a busty young blonde who is probably half his age, and he wanted to take a paid vacation and drag us along for the ride under the pretense of having a contact that claims..." She dropped off, feeling her entire body shake with anger and disgust. She'd already said too much to Beau. He was very easy to talk to. His voice and face made him seem trustworthy, and he was also charming and easygoing. So much so, that she'd let her guard down. Shaking her head, she took a deep breath to calm herself before finishing. "As I said, I'm just following orders."

CHAPTER THREE

Thirty miles west of the coast of Maui, he cut the engines and turned towards Nicky, who, after the short outburst about her boss, had grown extremely quiet. He figured that she'd released some emotions and information that she hadn't wanted to and was either embarrassed or frustrated at herself.

Either way, he'd enjoyed seeing her hold on those tight strings, which she no doubt had carefully put in place, flex. It made him want to rile her up again and see just how far she could cut loose.

"We're thirty miles out from the island," he said. She'd been frowning down at her phone for the past few minutes.

"I... don't have service." She motioned to her phone. "I can't seem to..."

"No cell towers out here," he said when she grew silent. "You'd need a satellite phone if you wanted to make calls." He held out his hand for the phone.

"I... had directions." She handed him her phone. "But can't seem to get to them."

"Are we there yet, boss?" Gordy asked as he came up the stairs.

"No, I can't get to the instructions Jake emailed me," Nicky told him.

Beau quickly connected her phone to the on-board satellite service that he paid for, then handed it back to her. "You're connected to service now."

"Oh good." She took the phone and then handed it back to him after a moment. "Here, we need to head here."

He looked at the coordinates and punched the numbers into his onboard GPS system before heading out again. "We're about ten minutes out," he told them.

"How's Leo handling the ride?" Nicky asked Gordy.

"He's sleeping," Gordy said with a shrug. "I've been enjoying the view from the back." Gordy sat in the other captain's chair across from Nicky.

"What happens when we arrive?" Beau asked them.

"Well, today," Nicky said, then she bit her bottom lip. "Not much. I wanted to come out here and..." She shrugged. "Look around. Maybe get used to the equipment. Assess the situation and get Gordy the training he needed."

"Today is a dry run for tomorrow," Gordy broke in. "Tomorrow, we meet our informant,"

"Jake's informant," Nicky interjected.

"Right, Jake's informant," Gordy corrected. "We'll meet him out here and start filming and, more important, dive down and find the treasure." He rubbed his hands together.

"Jake's informant claims he's found Lokelani's treasure already?" he asked, a little shocked.

"Apparently," Gordy answered, sounding excited. "He's hired us to document everything."

"I thought you did investigative journalism, not fiction?" Beau asked Nicky.

"She does," Gordy said, sounding frustrated. "Jake claims his informant has been harassed by...." At this point, Nicky elbowed him, and Gordy shut his mouth. "I think I'm going to go check on Leo." He quickly disappeared.

"Want to tell me what that was all about?" he asked Nicky when they were alone.

"No," she said easily with a smile. "For now, all you need to do is take us to the spot and get us in the water."

He thought about it for a moment and then figured that there was plenty of time to get more information from her or from Gordy. The man liked to talk. But it might be even more fun to break the walls that Nicky had put up.

"We're here," he said a few minutes later as he killed the engine and dropped the anchor.

Nicky leaned closer to the window and scanned the horizon as if expecting something.

"Want to get in the water?" he asked her.

"We could." She nodded slowly. "We had the resort pack us lunch. Maybe we should eat first?"

"Up to you, koa," he said casually and stood up. She smiled when he used the nickname. "The galley awaits." He motioned for her to head downstairs, then followed her.

Gordy and Leo apparently had the same idea as Nicky and were digging through the cooler they'd brought on board, pulling out the sandwiches and drinks that the resort had packed for them.

"Everything has mustard on it," Gordy complained. "I'm allergic to mustard seeds." He told Beau.

"The kitchen is pretty stocked. Help yourself to what you can find." He motioned to the fridge and cupboards.

As Gordy started looking for something else to eat, Nicky sat down and took a sandwich and a soda while going through their plans. She talked about an equipment check, both of the scuba gear and the recording gear. Then she talked about safety. He was going to go over that with them before letting them strap on any of the diving gear.

When they'd all finished lunch, they headed down to the main deck and started getting ready to get wet. While Nicky and Leo checked the scuba gear, he and Gordy carted up the needed camera equipment.

It took them three trips, but when they finally had everything Gordy claimed they needed, he started checking his own scuba equipment.

"Aren't you going to stay with the boat?" Nicky asked him.

"Yes, Gordy and I will be practicing and sticking close to the boat until I'm sure he's comfortable," he answered. "You and Leo, if you feel good about it, can head out."

She nodded. "Okay, for today, I think Leo and I won't be going too far." She narrowed her eyes. "Let's call it at half an hour," she suggested. "And we'll all stay within sight of the boat. For today."

"What about tomorrow?" Leo asked. "We will need—"

"We'll worry about tomorrow then," Nicky interrupted. "For today, you and I can check out the equipment and get used to the water and the new lighting equipment."

"Let me know what you need from me," Beau said.

"For now, just..." Leo motioned around. "Just helping with the equipment will do. Then you can get Gordy up to speed so we can use him the rest of the time."

For the next twenty minutes, he helped everyone gear up and double-checked equipment. Leo had changed at one point into a wet suit. Gordy was wearing board shorts like his own. When Nicky peeled off her shirt and skirt to reveal a sexy one-piece suit, he had a difficult time keeping his eyes off her as she slipped on her scuba gear.

Leo and Nicky slipped into the water almost an hour after he'd killed the engines and disappeared below the surface of the water. He checked his watch to time them.

"Now it's our turn," he told Gordy. "Just how comfortable are you in the water?"

The man wiggled his hand. "So, so."

"Let's see what you've got. We'll go down a few feet and swim around the boat. Let's take it nice and easy this first time out." He watched the man expertly flip into the water.

He slipped into the water and followed Gordy around, making sure the man knew how to check his equipment and oxygen levels, and keep his bearings.

This was the boring part of his job. When he took out inexperienced customers, he usually brought along Kailani's cousin Punahele and another one of her employees. Punahele was not only an expert scuba instructor, but he was also Beau's best friend.

The twenty-year-old was also skilled in flirting with hot tourists, which added to their tip percentage after a job.

But Punahele was on the Big Island currently, helping his mother move. Which meant Beau was all on his own.

He knew that Kailani wouldn't have sent him out on a job if she hadn't trusted him to keep clients safe. Still, he would have preferred knowing the skill levels of the three before letting them take off on their own. It made him nervous, waiting for the other two to surface. He kept checking his watch and listening to their chatter through the communication system in all of their full-face masks.

Kailani was not only a shrewd businesswoman, but she was also determined to have the best and the safest equipment. She upgraded all of their equipment every year. Customers seemed to appreciate the high-quality gear.

They were almost twenty minutes into the dive when he suggested to Gordy that they head back to the boat.

Just as they climbed out, they heard another boat approaching. This wasn't out of the norm. He knew most everyone around, so he waved at the coming vessel.

The smaller boat drew closer and stopped almost a hundred yards off his starboard side. A thin man in a baseball hat lifted a camera, snapped a few pictures of them, then gunned the engines and took off, heading back in the same direction he'd come.

"What was that all about?" he asked Gordy, but before the man answered, Leo surfaced, followed by Nicky.

"How'd it go down there?" he asked, helping Nicky climb up the ladder.

"Good, peaceful," she said, smiling.

It was the first time she'd looked relaxed since the first moment that he'd spotted her. Whatever else there was to her, she enjoyed diving and being in the water. This, he knew, they had in common.

He helped Leo out of the water next.

"We can take a short break and head back down. Leo wanted to check out some different equipment," Nicky said.

"Actually, I'll sit this one out," Leo said with a sigh. "Still a little jet lagged." He removed his oxygen tank and set it down.

"If you want, I'll go with you this time?" Beau offered.

Nicky's eyebrows shot up. "If it's okay with Leo to stay with the boat?"

"Sure, no problem," Leo said, dismissively.

"She's anchored, so we won't be going anywhere," Beau said.

"How'd Gordy do?" Nicky asked, sitting on one of the cushioned benches.

"Great. If he feels up to it, I think he's ready to head out with us. We can keep it to another half an hour if you want?" he asked the man.

"Sure thing," Gordy said, sounding excited.

Half an hour later, after they'd done another equipment check, swapped out their tanks, and drunk plenty of water, the three of them headed out together.

For the first few moments, he watched Gordy carefully. They were going deeper than they had earlier. Nicky had motioned to the depths and had headed directly below the boat.

Gordy hesitated for a split second, then followed Nicky straight down.

Diving was almost like riding a bike to him. It was work, sure, but feeling the water pressure cocoon you while enjoying the beauty of nature that surrounded you... well, there was really nothing else like it in the world.

Nicky seemed to know what she was doing. The moment they hit a reef, she turned and swam alongside it. She checked her gauges and even mentioned for Gordy to do the same.

She was so thorough at it that he wondered if she'd taught diving before.

Fifteen minutes into their dive, he noticed that there was a serious lack of shipwreck below them. If their informant had found Lokelani's treasure, it wasn't at the coordinates they'd given to Jake.

When they surfaced this time, he could tell that Nicky was growing frustrated. They had almost three hours before sunset and decided to call it a day.

Nicky stayed below deck with the rest of her coworkers while he drove them back to the island.

"If you want," he suggested after they had docked, "you

can keep all your equipment onboard. She's locked up at night, plus there's security at the docks."

"Thanks," Nicky said. She nodded to Leo. "Why don't you head in and get some rest. We'll be diving a lot longer tomorrow. We'll be heading out at first light."

"See you at six." Leo took off down the docks with Gordy carrying the cooler behind him.

"Disappointed?" he asked Nicky as she gathered her things.

She glanced up at him, her eyebrows arched. "No, it was as I suspected," she said with a slight sigh.

"So you think this is a wild goose chase?" he asked her, leaning on the railing.

"No, I think this is a farce." She started walking down the dock. "See you in the morning," she called over her shoulder.

CHAPTER FOUR

After a quick shower and a change of clothes, she put on a touch of makeup for her own vanity and headed downstairs to the dining room to meet with the rest of her team for an evening meeting that Jake had called.

It didn't surprise her to see the blonde at the bar, looking totally bored and sipping a glass of champagne.

Spotting the rest of her team, she made her way to the table and sat down. Jake gave her a look that clearly said he wasn't happy about her being late, but she brushed him off and ordered a glass of red wine and a shrimp salad, ignoring his looks.

"Leo and Gordy were just filling me in," Jake said. "It sounds like Gordy's ready for tomorrow and the equipment is good to go."

"Yes," she agreed as she sipped her water, waiting for the wine.

"What about the guide? Did you tell him anything?" Jake asked her.

"Anything?" She faked ignorance.

"About why we're out there?" Jake hissed.

"Oh, I think that any competent guide on the islands, who knows anything, would have guessed why we're thirty miles off the island. After all, it was all over the news last year when several items from Lokelani's treasure were found out there."

She remembered seeing pictures of the two Peruvian coins and several pieces of wood that had looked to her like nothing more than driftwood. Experts had declared with much fanfare that they were from the *Ukumari*, the boat that carried Lokelani's treasure to the islands back in the early eighteen hundreds.

"Right," Jake said slowly, "but how about the other part?"

"No," she said, frowning into her water. She hated leaving out the scariest part of their trip. As an investigative journalist, she didn't like leaving anyone in the dark about the dangers. Not that she thought there really would be any during this wild goose chase, but still. Beau should at least have a hint that there had supposedly been threats from powerful men who were out to stop them from filming.

"Good," Jake jumped in. He grew silent as her wine and salad were delivered.

As Jake went into the same speech about their mission that she'd already heard more than twice on this trip, she thought about Beau. She didn't know why, but her mind kept wandering to him all throughout the meeting and dinner.

The way he'd looked at her. How he'd looked just breathing. Okay, so maybe she had been focused on her career too much in the past few years.

It wasn't as if she had tried to let her personal life dry up. She'd been focused on getting ahead. In this field, she knew too many other journalists that had wavered in their focus and now were stay-at-home moms or secretaries to other journalists because they chose dating or marriage over going out and getting the story.

She supposed it wouldn't hurt to flirt a little. After all, she'd picked up instantly that Beau was interested in her.

What would it be like to have a fling while she was stuck there? She'd never had sex without some deeper connection before. Could she? Would she want to? Then her mind conjured up images of Beau and her entire body warmed. It would be fun trying at least.

She was smiling into her second glass of wine when Jake stood up and excused himself for the night, claiming he'd see them all in the morning and that they had better call it a night and get some rest themselves.

"It's not even nine o'clock," Gordy said with a sigh. "I'm heading to the bar." He wiggled his eyebrows. "See you all in the morning." He stood up and took his drink with him.

Nicky watched him smooth talk his way in between two women at the bar, who instantly laughed at something he said.

"I'm heading up," Leo added, taking the last two rolls from the basket. "Night." He left her alone at the table.

It was only then that she realized Jake hadn't paid for the meal. She pulled out her company card and waited for the check as she sipped her wine.

"That's a whole lot of empty plates. Tell me you didn't eat all that yourself," someone said from behind her.

She glanced over and smiled up at Beau.

"What would you say if I had?" she asked, motioning to the empty chair.

He chuckled as he sat down. "I'd be impressed." His eyes ran over her, and she felt her entire body heat again as she leaned on the table.

"You look good in clothes," she said, and only realized what she'd said after the words had left her mouth. Still, when his smile grew, she smiled back.

"Thanks, I think." He tilted his head slightly. "So do you."

She glanced down at the soft pink sundress she'd put on for the evening and then back at his button-up shirt and khaki pants.

"Have a hot date?" she asked him.

"No, just here to grab some dinner. You?"

"No, I had a boring business meeting, which has thankfully come to an end."

Just then the waitress walked over.

"Aloha, Beau," the woman said with a smile. "Your usual?"

Beau nodded, not really taking his eyes off Nicky. "Want to keep me company? I'll buy you another glass of wine."

"Sure, I won't turn down some dessert." She asked the sever for a menu.

"You won't need that," Beau said. "She'll have the chocolate lava cake." He looked back at her. "It's to die for."

She nodded. "Sounds perfect."

"I'll have a glass of what she's having too." He motioned to her empty wine glass.

After they had their wine, Beau asked, "How did the meeting go?"

"Boring." She rolled her eyes. "Jake treats us like children and explains everything several times. Your job must be nice. Taking new people out on the water each day. Not having a sniveling, cheating..." She shook her head. "Let's not talk about work." She leaned on the table and ran her eyes over his face, then locked eyes with him. "Do you live close by?"

"No, I'll be staying on the *Ho'omau* while I'm helping you out."

"You're staying on your boat?" She thought about him sleeping in the main cabin that she'd seen earlier.

"It makes it easier." He shrugged. "How are you liking your room here?"

"It's a small room," she answered. "I have a view of the parking lot." She groaned.

"That won't do." He frowned. "I can pull some strings?"

She was about to deny him, but then smiled. "It'll make Jake angry if I have a better view than him. He specifically asked that our rooms be on the north side of the building. I know for a fact his room is facing the water."

"What kind of boss does that?" he asked.

"One that doesn't want his employees to see his mistress sneaking in and out of his room." She narrowed her eyes at him when she realized she didn't know if Beau was married or seeing someone seriously. Did it matter? Yes. If she wanted to feel free to flirt with him for the remainder of her time there, she had to know. "What about you? Are you seeing someone? Married?"

"Neither. You?"

She shook her head as his food was delivered and her dessert was set in front of her. "Are you thinking what I'm thinking?" he asked, his voice low and almost a purr.

An image of them up in her room, her pinned against the wall as he took her mouth and... the rest of her, flashed in her mind.

"Hm?" she asked, totally breathless.

"That you'll have to save me a bite of that," he finished with a smile.

She looked down at the massive chocolate brownie, which was topped with two scoops of ice cream and covered in hot fudge, nuts, and chocolate flakes.

"What'll you give me in return?" she asked. She heard his breath catch.

Okay, so the three glasses of wine were making her a little more relaxed than she normally was. Flirting with him came easily.

"Don't answer that." She held up her hand. "I'm too drunk to think straight. Eat." She motioned to his food.

"Too bad," he said. "I love to negotiate."

"So..." She took a bite of the dessert and then moaned with pleasure. She couldn't remember the last time she'd tasted anything as rich and sweet.

"Yeah, it's the best on all the islands," Beau said, breaking into her thoughts. "What did you want to say?" he asked when she didn't finish her thought.

"Oh, right," she said after another bite. "So, you're ex-military." It was a statement, not a question. Beau nodded his head, and that dark look was back in his eyes. "It's obvious something happened." Again, she held up her hand. "I'm not asking for details. I've known a lot of veterans and understand not to butt in."

"I appreciate that," he said smoothly. "Do you have a family member that served?"

She shook her head. "No, an ex," she admitted, causing his eyebrows to rise.

"Recent ex?" he asked, and she smiled.

"Recent enough."

"Was it serious?"

She shook her head. "Not after he tried to kill me," she admitted dryly. She took another bite of the chocolate.

"Which is a story for another day." She didn't want to darken the mood any further.

Normally she refrained from getting drunk. At home, a couple glasses of wine would have just given her a slight buzz. Tonight, however, after spending the entire day in the sun, she was just tired enough that the extra glass was making her mind spin. She was all over the place. One minute she was thinking about hot, steamy sexy with Beau, and the next the hell James had put her through.

She hated thinking about the eight-month-long relationship that had ended abruptly one night almost four months ago.

She'd done enough pieces on PTSD to know James was a prime candidate the moment they had started dating. Still, she'd given the guy a chance. After all, his outward appearance assured her that he had it all together. He was a very successful business owner. He owned three local gyms in San Francisco and was opening another one when they met.

James owned his own lavish home in Nob Hill and drove around the city in a custom Corvette. Outwardly, he'd had his shit together.

It wasn't until they'd been dating almost five months that the controlling monster that lurked inside had been exposed.

"Okay, later. But I'll want to know the guy's name and where I can find him to kick his ass," Beau said easily, making her smile.

"Deal." She laughed and took another bite of her chocolate, instantly forgetting about James. "What about you? Any skeletons in your closet?"

His eyes locked with hers. "I don't hit or threaten women. Ever." His voice was low, and he looked into his eyes. She could see it was the truth. Whatever ghosts lurked behind his dark eyes, controlling and abusing people weaker than him was not one of them.

She nodded. "Not every man is James," she agreed. "I meant crazy ex-girlfriends."

He relaxed a little. "Nope, I've been single too long. Or so Kailani, Keone, and Alana keep telling me. They're basically my *'ohana.*" He shrugged. "I'm sure you'll meet the rest of them during your stay on the islands."

"You mentioned that you've known Kailani since you were young?" she asked.

He nodded. "When I returned, I purchased my home from Mateo, Kailani's brother. He was my best friend growing up. He's currently stationed in Europe." Beau smiled. "Married over there and does not intend to return, so he gave me a good deal."

"Is he the one you purchased the boat from too?"

Beau's eyebrows shot up. "No, that was Matt, Kailani's husband. Matt likes to buy new things every year. When he purchased a new boat last Christmas, I got the old one at a steal."

"What does Matt do?" she asked.

Beau leaned closer to her, close enough that she could smell his aftershave. The musky scent was better than that of the melted fudge on her brownie.

"He owns this resort," he said with a smile. "Which is why I'm sure that I can get you the best room available for your entire stay. In exchange for..." Her breath hitched as thoughts of sex with him played in her head. Her body vibrated with want. "A bite of that brownie," he finished with a smile.

CHAPTER FIVE

There was nothing better than seeing the obvious look of jealousy on her boss's face in the morning. He was positive that Nicky had bragged about the new private bungalow that she had been moved into after dinner the night before.

He could almost guarantee that she had left out the part where he'd been the one to get her room changed. It hadn't taken much, and he didn't even have to get Matt involved since everyone at the resort knew him so well and knew his connection to the family.

He'd enjoyed the look on her face when she'd stepped into the little bungalow directly off the beach. He had even helped her lug her suitcase down the path, past the pool, and into the one-room bungalow, but then he'd quickly told her he had an early morning and left.

He'd wanted to kiss her. To see just how soft she felt pressed up against him. But she'd had three glasses of wine, so he'd walked out without so much as a glance backwards.

Now, he steered the *Ho'omau* out into open water, with Nicky's boss sitting directly beside him, glaring out the windshield. He knew the man was upset about something and figured it was probably the bungalow.

Nicky was sitting on the other side of Beau, looking smug and relaxed. If she'd rubbed her new lodgings in the man's face, Beau had a little more respect for her. After all, the man had gone out of his way to insult Beau no fewer than five times before they had even left the dock. Beau wanted to rub the man's nose in something himself.

"You're sure you know where we're heading?" Jake asked for the tenth time.

"Yes. I've locked the GPS coordinates into the system." He motioned to his onboard computer. "If you want, you can head down and relax. It will take us about forty minutes to get there."

"I'll wait here," Jake said firmly. "I want to make sure you don't waver from the course."

Beau grunted in response and leaned back, trying to look bored. He wasn't going to let the man get under his skin. Over the past few years, many men had tried and, so far, none had succeeded.

Nicky leaned back and slipped on a pair of sunglasses. He wanted to talk to her like they had the day before, but since Jake was there, he remained silent. The only sound was the engine of the boat and the salt water being pushed out of its way.

When they finally arrived at the coordinates, Nicky appeared to be asleep and Jake was seriously close to breaking through Beau's chill factor.

He cut the engine and dropped anchor, then met everyone on the back deck. Like yesterday, he went through the standard checklist and checks of equipment. Only this time, Jake interjected each time and explained or countered everything he said, as if his employees were idiots who had never gone diving before.

"The man can seriously get on one's nerves," he said under his breath to Nicky, who nodded in response before slipping on her oxygen tank.

"You're sure you'll stay with the boat?" Jake asked, causing Beau's eyebrows to rise. "It's just... I've heard a few reports of guides taking paying customers out to the middle of nowhere and leaving them. Then demanding ransom—"

"I'll stay," he said firmly. Jake seemed to get his warning tone and nodded before falling backwards into the water.

"He's an ass," Leo said before slipping on his mask and jumping off the boat.

"But he signs our checks," Gordy added before putting on his own mask and falling into the water.

"See you in an hour," Nicky said. He stopped her from jumping into the water by taking her hand.

"I thought you were supposed to rendezvous with Jake's informant?" he asked, looking around. Currently, there was no other boat in sight.

"We were." Nicky frowned. "Jake wouldn't give us any further information other than the new directions we're supposed to dive to."

"Care to let me in on where you're going? In case?" he asked.

She glanced towards the water and sighed. "There's a reef. We swam along it yesterday. We're supposed to go about a mile into the reef. There's a cave."

"Tell me you're not going in a cave," he said firmly.

"I'm not," she assured him. "I'm not comfortable enough to go inside, and Leo is claustrophobic." She bit her lip and glanced towards the water. "I'd better..." She motioned to the water, and he dropped her hand.

"I'll be here." He watched her slip below the water.

Was Jake really going to dive inside a cave? Did the man have enough experience? Reef caves were nothing like natural caves. More dangers lurked in the sharp narrow passages carved out of the reefs.

An hour and a half later, the first diver surfaced. He wanted to berate them for cutting it so close. The tanks would be running low or even on reserve.

One by one they surfaced, and it was only after he saw Nicky swimming towards him that he relaxed.

"How'd it go?" he asked her. She gave him a look, then quickly shook her head as Jake climbed on board.

"That was a colossal waste of time," Jake said, tossing down his face mask.

Beau wanted to remind the guy that it was rented equipment and that the masks cost a few thousand dollars each, but instead, he picked it up and helped Jake remove his tank and the rest of the equipment before he could break anything.

"Maybe your guy was—" Leo started, but Jake hissed at him, then looked directly at Beau.

The entire group was silent. Beau could feel the awkwardness as he continued to secure the equipment.

"We'll break for lunch, then head back down," Jake said as he pulled out his cell phone. He stepped inside and shut the door behind him, then he started talking to someone on the phone.

"What was that all about?" he asked Nicky quietly.

"A whole lot of nothing." She rolled her eyes. "First, apparently, his contact was a no-show this morning. Jake claimed he gave us detailed directions to the site, but..."

"There's a whole lot of nothing down there. I know, I got caught up in the hunt last year." He smiled.

"You did?"

"Who wouldn't? The chance at millions?" He shrugged. "I joined in the search and spent a few free hours diving along with the rest of them. Never found anything except for shells and sand."

Nicky's eyes moved towards the door where Jake had disappeared to, then over to her colleagues.

Leo shrugged while Gordy looked down at his fingernails.

"We're here to do a job. I can't investigate if there's nothing here." She motioned around.

"It's better than sitting in the office back home," Gordy suggested, causing Nicky's eyes to narrow.

"Paid vacation," Leo added. "It's why I took the job twenty-some years ago." He started walking towards the cabin and threw over his shoulder, "Beats sitting behind a desk."

Gordy followed him inside, but Beau waited while Nicky slipped on her shorts and pulled her long-wet hair into a ponytail.

"Something tells me you'd never sit behind a desk," he said, leaning against the railing.

She glanced up at him and rolled her eyes. "I tried it once." She tilted her head. "I can't see you behind a desk either."

He chuckled. "Nope, never tried it. Except at school. My teachers claimed I had ADHD, but the truth of it is I'm in my element out here." He motioned around.

She smiled. "I can see that."

"Not that I got bad grades," he added, feeling his face heat. "Straight A's," he said with pride.

"I can see that too." She nodded. "I was the one who was always sticking my nose where it shouldn't have been. I had one of my teachers complain that I asked too many questions. Of course, she was only complaining since I found out she'd been sleeping with the married gym teacher." She wiggled her eyebrows. He smiled as she stood up and stretched. "Still, Leo and Gordy are right, this does beat being back home." She took in a deep breath and stepped inside.

Instead of joining the four of them for lunch, he went back upstairs and sat alone looking out over the water. At one point, he could hear raised voices below deck and thought about heading down to check and see if everything was okay, but then the voices died down.

He used his time alone to do a little research on his phone. He looked into the company Nicky worked for, read a couple articles she'd written, and watched a few of her reports.

Gordy was right. She was good at her job. Very good.

He looked at a long list of her past jobs and was wondering why she'd been chosen for this story when her stories leaned more towards corporate and environmental misdeeds. She had the occasional heartstrings report about some injustice to families or a missing person's case.

This story seemed more in line with what one of her coworkers, a Rebecca Light, usually reported on. The middle-aged woman was all over the treasure-hunting type of articles.

"Do you have a moment?" Nicky interrupted his search on his phone. Setting his phone down, he turned to her.

"Sure," he said, motioning to the chair beside his.

"Why are there three captain's chairs?" she asked, sitting down beside him.

He smiled. "There's only one captain's chair." He

patted the middle one that sat in front of the controls. "The others are for the co-captain and navigators."

"Right."

"I heard some raised voices," he said when she stared out the windshield quietly.

She sighed heavily. "Jake wants Gordy to go deeper into the cave during our next dive."

"No," he said quickly with a frown. "The kid has only gone diving four times. He's not experienced enough for a cave dive. Hell, he's not even experienced enough to swim in coral like what's below." He thought of the skinny guy trying to fight the strong currents that went through some of the coral reefs that he'd dived in before.

"I agree. So does Leo, but Jake is determined that someone go in and have a look around." Nicky leaned back in the chair.

"What does Gordy think?" he asked her.

"Gordy thinks he's capable, but then again, he's a twenty-year-old male, ego and all. He started as an intern just last year and moved up quickly, so he's a talented guy. But I'm not sure about his diving skills."

His eyes narrowed. "I can't allow it." He stood up. She followed him back downstairs where Jake, Leo, and Gordy were all preparing to go out again.

"Nicky tells me you're going into the cave?" he asked Gordy.

The guy glanced sideways at Jake, before nodding his head. "Someone's got to."

Beau turned to Jake. "Sorry, it's my call as captain. Brody is too inexperienced. I'm not going to allow it. Not until he's had a few more hours diving."

Jake chuckled "You're not going to... allow it?" He shook his head. "He is my employee. You've been hired to chauffer us out here. That's all." Jake handed Gordy an almost-empty oxygen tank.

Beau stepped forward and stopped the guy from pulling it on. "Always check your own equipment," he said firmly. "This tank is almost empty. It would have gotten you to the bottom, where you would have stayed." He turned to Jake. "While you're under my care, what I say goes," he said firmly. He looked back to Gordy. "You won't be diving again today. One deep dive a day is enough for someone with your experience."

Jake's eyes narrowed, and Beau could see the man's back teeth actually grinding.

"Fine," he said slowly. "If he can't go, then you'll do it. After all, what exactly are we paying you for?"

He was about to remind the guy that he was just a chauffeur, but then he figured the only way to shut the guy up was to do it himself.

Without saying anything more, he started getting ready for the dive, making sure to slip on his wet suit. The extra layer could save you from scrapes and cuts when swimming through the sharp coral.

"I go in. No one else." He glanced towards Nicky.

"Nope." Jake shook his head. "I'm going in first. You're just backup."

"I don't know your skill level," he told Jake.

"And I don't know yours. I guess you'll just have to keep up with me to find out." Jake slipped on his mask and jumped into the water.

Beau was right behind him, but not before making sure Nicky and Leo were in first.

"Don't touch anything," he told Gordy before jumping in.

It took him a little while to catch up with Jake. Not that the guy was fast, but he'd had a head start on him.

Nicky and Leo followed more closely, Leo carting the big underwater camera, while Nicky carried an extra camera and lighting equipment.

He didn't know if they were filming the entire time. His focus was on keeping up with Jake.

When they entered the coral fields, he was slightly surprised when it appeared as if the man knew where he was going. The coral was like a maze. Jake swam around large sections of it, under natural arches made from dark lava rocks topped with colorful coral.

A huge green turtle darted out from under a rock, shot off to the left, and quickly disappeared. He wanted to laugh when it spooked Jake so badly the man jerked in response. When he recovered, however, he continued on until they came to a deeper section.

They swam until they reached a section of tabletop coral. It was called that because it sat just above the ocean floor and fanned out like it was the top of a massive table. Underneath was the soft sand, while above was the hard surface of jagged rocks.

Normally, you wouldn't swim underneath a large section of it, as it was easy to get turned around and possibly trapped underneath. Like getting trapped under the ice in a frozen lake. But Jake took off between the sections and he, Nicky, and Leo followed behind.

When they came to the actual cave, it was nothing more than a hole between the top coral and a section of lava rock.

Jake turned to him and pointed. "This is it. Ready?" he asked, but before Beau could respond, he took off into the hole.

"Stay here," he told Nicky and Leo.

"Here." Nicky shoved the camera she had into his hands. She reached over and flipped on the bright light attached to it. "It's running."

He nodded and took off after Jake, squeezing between the hard rocks. His tank bumped against the coral and all he could see was Jake's flippers in front of him in the darkness.

It took a long time to snake their way through the narrow passage. He wondered just how far the man was going to take them and kept checking his gauges and watch.

Less than five minutes after entering the cave, the bottom dropped out and opened up into a chasm. Jake stopped and looked around for a moment before heading straight down, into the darkness.

Beau had to admit it, the man had balls, going blindly into the darkness in a cave he'd supposedly never been in before.

Less than fifteen feet below, there were three tunnels that shot off from the main area. Jake pointed to the far right one and suddenly Beau realized that this wasn't Jake's first time in the cave.

Nicky had claimed that no one had entered the cave during their earlier dive that day. Which meant Jake had been here before. There was no way the man would know exactly where he was going without being here at least once before now.

Beau followed Jake until the cave narrowed and the man's oxygen tank started hitting the coral above them, stopping their forward motion.

"Son of a..." Jake said. He jerked free and, in the process, pulled his tank all the way off. Beau watched as the he jerked around, desperate for air.

CHAPTER SIX

Nicky waited with Leo at the mouth of the cave. The only thing keeping her calm was the steady sound of her breathing. Occasionally, a fish would dart by, but her eyes were locked on the dark spot where Jake and Beau had disappeared.

It had been so kind of Beau to arrange for her new room. Room? Heck, he'd upgraded her to a full bungalow all to herself. It was one of a dozen the resort had that sat on a private path away from the main resort, just off the sand and overlooking the water.

On one side, she had large glass doors overlooking the beach and on the other a private patio surrounded by thick, lush greenery and views of the swimming pool. The room had everything a Hawaiian trip should have—a huge canopy bed, a massive jacuzzi bathtub, and its very own private hammock overlooking the beach. She was looking forward to spending time in that very soon.

If Beau ever came back. The worry surfaced again, and she glanced down at her watch and gauges. They'd been gone for more than half an hour.

What would she do if something went wrong? She knew that cave diving was a lot different than open water diving. The currents in the coral could be tricky, not to mention marine life. White-tip reef sharks were not uncommon. She'd spotted more than a dozen of them just in the few dives they'd taken already. For the most part, they were more spooked of humans than humans were of them, but still, it wasn't uncommon for great whites or hammerheads to be lurking in the water either. Then there were the tiger sharks. She glanced around and felt herself shiver. Those were the ones she'd been told to watch out for. They were wicked aggressive and, out of all the videos she'd watched in preparation for diving, they were the ones that scared her the most.

She lost track of time and realized she hadn't been checking her gauges as much as she should have. Finally, she relaxed as a dim light appeared in the darkness, signaling the return of Beau and Jake.

When she noticed that it was Jake that was carrying the camera and light, she panicked until she noticed Beau right behind him.

"Up," Beau said firmly, and everyone started heading back to the boat.

Beau was the last one out of the water and, just like before, Jake tossed his mask and tank down on the deck and stormed off to make another call.

"We're done here," Beau said firmly, picking up the equipment and putting it away.

"Problems?" she asked when they were alone.

"He's not allowed on my boat again," Beau said in a low voice.

He didn't look angry as much as disappointed. Then

again, she didn't really know his looks, so it could have been both.

"What happened down there?" she asked him when they were alone.

"The man is reckless with his own life. I doubt he or Gordy would have surfaced if they'd gone into that cave alone," he growled out, his eyes on the man standing just inside the large back windows.

Nicky turned to look at Jake, who appeared to be screaming into his phone. As they both watched, Jake tossed his phone across the room, no doubt shattering it and anything else in its path.

"I want him off my boat," Beau said, "and I can guarantee you that no one else on the island will take him out on the water." Beau walked inside and she followed. Without saying anything to any of the rest of them, he climbed the stairs.

She was about to follow, but Jake took her arm. "We'll go back down," he started to say, but then they heard the anchor being lifted and the motor kicking on. "Where the hell does he think we're going?" Jake let go of her arm and marched up the stairs.

"I have never seen him so…" Leo started to say, but then they all jumped when the shouting started.

She was the first one up the stairs, followed by Gordy.

"I don't give a shit. I've hired you and what I say goes. We are staying put." Jake yanked the throttle back, jerking the boat and everyone on it forward as they stopped.

"Touch the controls again and you'll be swimming back to Maui," Beau said in a calm voice.

"Is that a threat?" Jake pushed himself directly in Beau's face. The fact that her boss was more than twenty years older than Beau and almost a foot shorter didn't stifle the look of pure rage in Jake's eyes.

Beau, for his part, looked as if he'd calmed himself down since they'd returned to the surface.

"That's a promise. I'll still take your crew out, but you're grounded. No one else on the island will allow you to step foot on their vessel. That's another promise." Beau reached over and slowly moved the throttle so the boat was once again heading back to the island.

"What I say..." Jake reached past Beau for the throttle, but this time, he ended up on his ass almost five feet away. The man actually slid on the hardwood flooring, his wet shorts making a squeegee sound.

"If I have to, I'll call the coast guard to come pick you up." Beau sat down in the chair and nudged the throttle until the boat was speeding across the water.

Both Nicky and Gordy watched Jake, unsure of what the man would do next. Obviously, he'd taken a hit to his manhood, being tossed down like a spoiled child who hadn't gotten his way.

In the three years she'd worked with him, she'd never seen him not get what he wanted. Well, except when she'd turned his advances down during that first Christmas party. After that, his entire attitude towards her had changed. He'd gone out of his way to stifle her career. Any advancements she'd made were in spite of his direct actions to stop her forward motion.

Without a word, Jake got up from the floor and disappeared down the stairs, but not before glaring at the back of Beau's head.

"Wow," Gordy said under his breath. "I wonder who is going to pay for that?" He turned as if to follow Jake downstairs, but then thought better of it and stepped out on the upper deck instead. She watched him sit on the long bench and watch the waves caused by the motor.

"Are you okay?" she asked Beau, taking the seat next to him.

"Me?" His eyebrows went up slightly. "Perfect. You?" His eyes ran over her. When he frowned, she followed his gaze to where Jake had grabbed her arm and noticed the perfect outline of his fingers on her skin.

"Don't get excited," she told Beau, touching his arm when he jerked to stand up. "I was chilled from the dive." She rubbed her arms and within a few seconds, the marks disappeared. "You probably can't tell it, but I'm very fair skinned. I bruise easily too. All I have to do is bump into a table and you'd swear someone hit me with a baseball bat." She chuckled and then relaxed when Beau leaned back in the chair.

"Right," he said, watching the horizon.

"Thank you," she said softly.

"For?" he asked, not taking his eyes from the view.

"For not killing my boss," she joked.

Beau glanced over at her. "It's been a while since I've wanted to kill someone," he said with a shrug.

She smiled. "An ex?" She leaned closer, folding her legs and resting her elbows on her knees.

Beau shifted slightly. "No, one of Keone's exes."

"Oh?" She nudged his leg when he stopped talking.

"His name was Earl. Who names their kid Earl and doesn't know that the guy is going to grow up to be a jerk?" Beau rolled his eyes.

"My father's name is Earl," she said easily, and he winced. Laughing, she shook her head. "I'm joking. His name is Lorenzo." Beau chuckled. "My mother's name is Camilla. But everyone calls her Cammy and my dad, Papa

Cardone. They own a restaurant back home. But go on. What did Earl do to make you want to kill him? He didn't hurt Keone, did he?"

"The fact that that is the first place you go tells me we need to have that talk about your ex, James, very soon," Beau said.

She was slightly surprised that he remembered her ex's name. Or the conversation at all. She'd been tipsy and hadn't meant to tell him all that.

"What did Earl do?" she asked, trying to keep the conversation off her past.

"He stole my boat, threw a huge party. Trashed it pretty good. I had to repaint..." He stopped himself and shook his head. "Keone hadn't been invited and found out a few weeks later that the girl he'd cheated on her with during the party was pregnant."

"Yeah, I'd like to throttle the jerk too," she said easily.

"What kind of restaurant?" he asked her.

"Our last name is Cardone, so naturally... Mexican." She smiled.

He laughed. "Did you inherit any skills?" he asked with a smile.

"Some, why?" She felt her heart kick in her chest.

"I have the fixings for some chicken parmesan in the kitchen downstairs. If you want, we could skip the crowded dining experience tonight?" he asked, and she felt her insides start to heat.

"I might be persuaded, if you have anything close to that lava cake for dessert," she said with a low purr.

He reached over and took her hand in his. "I can guarantee it if you say yes."

She nodded, then heard shouting downstairs. When

Beau moved to stand up, she put a hand on his shoulder. "No, don't. I'll handle this."

He nodded and she stood up and made her way down the stairs.

The moment she made it to the bottom of the stairs, she realized that Leo was the chosen one for all of Jake's anger.

"I don't give a shit if you're allergic to coral. I'll tell you" —Jake shoved a finger into Leo's chest— "where to dive and you'll go. That's how this all works."

"No, not this time," Leo said, glancing towards her. "Neither will Gordy. As Beau said, he's not ready."

"You and Nicky will—" Jake started.

Nicky stepped forward, getting Jake's attention.

"No, we won't. SWE pays us to do a job, not to head into a situation that we know is stupidly dangerous." She crossed her arms over her chest. "Beau says that if he hadn't been there, neither you nor Gordy would have returned from the dive today."

"He doesn't know shit," Jake spat back. "I've been diving longer than he's been out of diapers."

She wanted to argue, but instead just shrugged. "Either way, it's his boat. His island. He knows everyone and, according to him, you crossed the line today."

Jake was quiet for a moment. "I doubt he knows everyone. Besides, the company paid him a lot of money to guide us. Once I have a nice little chat with his boss..."

"Oh, you mean his best friend's sister, Kailani?" she asked with a smirk. "Whose husband owns the resort we're staying in?"

Jake's eyes narrowed slightly. "Then we'll go somewhere else. Honolulu isn't far—"

"Would you just stop." She threw up her hands. "I get

it. You want someone to go into that cave. What about your contact?" she asked.

Jake's eyes narrowed even more. "I haven't heard from him. Not since..." He shook his head.

"Okay, so..." She started pacing, moving with the rocking of the boat. She stopped pacing. "We get Beau to train us. Gordy and myself." She glanced over at Leo.

"We don't have time," Jake hissed.

"Why not? It's not like there are a million other boats looking." She motioned to the empty waters around them. "Starting tomorrow," she suggested.

Jake was quiet for a while. "It might work. I could..."

"Nope, you're grounded. Or...landlocked." She shrugged. "Either way, I'm pretty sure Beau is going to see to it that you won't be allowed on the water again." Jake glared towards the stairs. "Just... let us do what you pay us for. I'm sure we'll be exploring that cave in no time."

Jake was silent for a while, then he growled out, "I've got a call to make." He glanced around and spotted his phone on the floor. He picked it up, and sure enough, the screen was cracked, but he stepped out the door and started talking on it. Either he was faking it, or his phone still worked.

"Think he's going to go for it?" Leo asked softly. She knew he wasn't talking about Jake, but about Beau.

"There's only one way to find out." She thought about heading up there and asking him right then, but then figured the better plan would be to wait until later that night after he'd had some of the best chicken parmesan in his life.

CHAPTER SEVEN

By the time they docked, it was only two hours until sunset. He had a quick word with Kailani over the radio before docking and wasn't surprised that she was there to meet them when they got to shore. She stepped on the boat and, with a smile, asked to speak to Jake privately.

He knew better than to see if Kailani wanted or needed his help. If she did, she'd yell loud enough to alert the entire island. So, he started his post-docking checklist and began cleaning up, starting in the kitchen area.

Either Gordy or Leo had already stored the camera and other gear down below deck before disembarking. Nicky helped him clean up the mess left behind from lunch and then helped him load up the empty oxygen tanks on the cart so they could be exchanged for fresh ones in the morning before they headed out again.

"You do this every day?" Nicky asked him as he started scrubbing the deck with a broom and the hose from the docks.

"Every day that I take a group out."

"How often do you do that?"

"Normally?" He thought about it for a moment. "A couple times a month."

"That's all?" she asked with a frown. "Do most groups go out for days?"

He shook his head. "Most just go out a day or two. Some, the ones that want to sail around the islands and sleep in the boat, will go out for a few nights."

She was quiet for a moment. "So, this isn't really a full-time job for you then, is it?"

He frowned as he thought about it. "It's not really a job. It's more like..."

"Beau is helping a friend out," Kailani broke in as she stepped out onto the dock with Jake directly behind her.

The fact that the man was smiling had Beau relaxing slightly.

"Beau doesn't need to work," Kailani finished, more for Jake's benefit than for Nicky's, he was sure. "After everything he did for our country, he's set for life," she added with a wink. "It's all you now," she added under her breath as she passed him. Then she said, "Pōmaika'i iā 'oe," which meant, good fortune, Hawaii's version of good luck.

Jake passed by him without a single word, but then stopped and turned when he was about ten feet away. "Come along, Nicky."

The man was actually calling her like a dog. He glanced over and saw Nicky's eyebrows arch upwards.

"I'll finish helping clean up. You go along. I'm sure you have plenty to do." She turned away and dismissed hm.

"You handled that well," he said when they were alone.

"That man is..." She took a deep breath. "A blessing," she said with a forced grin.

"Right." He laughed.

They worked side by side, cleaning the deck until every-thing was back to normal.

"I guess I never realized how messy Gordy and Leo could be," she said when he tossed a large bag of trash into the bin on the dock.

"Most of it was from Jake. At least I assume." He shrugged. "Yesterday it wasn't as bad."

"Right." Nicky sighed. "What time would you like me around for dinner?" she asked.

He thought about it. "Now is good."

She laughed. "It's only..." She glanced down at her watch. "How did it get to be seven already?"

He smiled. "Time flies..."

"When you're cleaning," she finished with a chuckle. "Lead the way." She motioned to the boat, and he once again helped her climb aboard.

He stepped into the kitchen and started pulling out the necessary ingredients.

Most nights on board, he'd settle for a cold sandwich or a microwave dinner. But after bumping into Nicky last night in the restaurant, he'd headed to the store and purchased a few things with the intention of inviting her on board for dinner.

He hadn't planned on her making it. But after he started preparing the meal, she nudged him aside, bumping her hip against his.

"You pour us some wine. Let the full-blooded Italian do her thing in here," she said in a thick Italian accent as she wiggled her eyebrows.

"I wouldn't want to get in the way." He pulled out a bottle of red wine he'd purchased to go with the meal. "Does this meet with your approval?" He showed her the label.

She looked surprised. "I know that family." She tapped the label. "I've actually been to the winery more times than I can count." She sighed. "If I was at my cousin's wedding today, I'm sure I'd have my fill of it there."

"Small world." He opened the bottle. "There are a handful of reds I like. This is one of them." He poured them each a glass.

"My brother is there right now." She moved around the small kitchen like she'd cooked in it many times before.

"Where? The winery?" he asked, sitting down and watching her.

"No." She smiled over her shoulder. "My cousin's wedding. Venice." She sighed. "Apparently, so is his best friend and lifelong crush, Claire."

"Oh?" He leaned on the bar top.

"Yes. I think my mother had something to do with that. Claire had always talked about her dream trip to Italy. Ever since we took one of our yearly trips when we were kids, and she tried to stow away in my brother's suitcase." Nicky laughed. "Claire is no contortionist. Anyway, my mother convinced Claire to take the trip at the same time Isabella's wedding was taking place, then Cammy supposedly twisted her ankle jumping off the sofa so my parents had to stay home and it would just be my brother." She stopped and rolled her eyes. "Not very subtle if you ask me, but then again, Cammy has never been one for subtlety." She stopped and smiled at him. "Nudge, nudge." She motioned with her hands. "Cammy is great for nudging people into relationships. It's just funny that those two didn't get together sooner. You know the type." She continued talking as she worked, and he was completely mesmerized by her cooking skills and by the way she moved.

The soft blue sundress she was wearing over her swim-suit flowed with each step she made in the small kitchen.

By the time she slid the pan of chicken into the oven, he knew all about her brother Justin, who was gearing up to take over the family's restaurant, A Taste of Italy, back in Castle Rock, Colorado. And Claire Stein, a clothing designer that they had known and lived next to since... forever.

Claire was the younger sister of Robin Stein, the movie actress. He'd seen a few movies with the star in them but didn't know anything about her personally. From what he could remember, she was beautiful and a really great actress.

"So, what about you?" he asked. When her eyebrows shot up, he added, "Did she ever nudge you into a rela-tionship?"

She chuckled. "The question is, when *didn't* she nudge me." She rolled her eyes. "Any good-looking available man that walked through TTOI's doors, she gave them my number or set up a date. Or at least tried to. After a while, I threatened to never give her grandkids, and she backed off." She turned and went to work on some sort of oil sauce then she slid the bread he'd purchased into the oven on a plate as she continued talking about her family.

For a moment, he completely lost himself in her stories. She made him laugh when she told him funny things that her brother had done in their youth. He could see the obvious love for her family and for Claire as well.

He wondered if she knew that she already thought of the woman as family?

"What about you?" she said after a moment of quiet.

"Me?" He poured them each more wine.

"Family?" she asked, leaning against the counter and looking at him.

He thought for a moment about the family he'd lost that day several years ago. The family he had now here in Maui. Then he answered. "Besides my mother and Carl, I have a step-sister, Kara." He admitted. "She's twenty-years-old lives in Wyoming and works on her father's massive ranch."

"I always wanted a younger sister," Nicky said with a slight sigh. "My parents claimed they had too much to handle with my brother and I." She chuckled. "Still, every trip we took to Italy to visit family, I came home thankful that it was just the two of us. All those cousins." She rolled her eyes. "Half of the time I didn't even know how I was related to most of them. Still don't." She laughed as she sipped the glass of wine. "When were you in Italy?" she asked suddenly.

"A few years before..." He shook his head, realizing he was about to tell her about that day. "A few years ago," he said instead.

Nicky's eyes narrowed. "You do remember what I do for a living, right?"

"Yeah," he answered and took a sip of his wine. "Why?"

"Before?" she said, motioning with her wine. When he remained quiet, she shrugged. "Too soon?"

He thought about telling her. It wasn't that he didn't trust her with the story. Or that he didn't want to tell her. But it would be the first time he'd told anyone except for the mandatory shrink he'd seen for the first year.

"No," he said softly.

"Not enough wine then?" she asked, and once again he thought about it.

"The story shouldn't be told. Ever. But I'll settle for after we eat."

"Fair enough." She walked over to the small oven and checked the chicken. The scent that billowed out with the heat had his stomach growling loudly. He was pretty sure it smelled better than anything that had ever been cooked in that kitchen before.

"If that tastes half as good as it smells, I might just have to hire you on as my personal chef," he joked.

Nicky laughed and shook her head. "I like to cook, but if I wanted to do it for a living, I would have stayed home in Colorado. Besides, I'm good, but my father and brother are a million times better."

He helped her set the small table and, once the food was ready, he carted everything over for her while she finished up with the bread.

"Saluto," she said, tapping her glass to his. "Buon appetito."

It only took one bite for him to realize that it was the best chicken parmesan he'd ever had in his life.

"Well?" she asked after his third bite without saying anything.

"Can't talk," he mumbled. "Stuffing my face with the best meal I've had in my entire life."

She chuckled. "I'll take the compliment." She continued eating.

When he'd finished his plate, he brought the pan back to the table with him and scooped another helping onto his plate and hers.

He'd totally forgotten about the bread and took a chunk of it as well. When he bit into it, he frowned and looked at it. "How the hell did you get it to taste so good? It's store-bought bread."

She laughed again. "Garlic, oil, salt." She shrugged. "You had limited spices here."

"Best meal ever," he said, pausing between each word. "We should negotiate you cooking each night during your stay."

He was too busy eating the excellent meal to realize that she'd stopped eating and was just watching him.

CHAPTER EIGHT

Watching Beau enjoy the dinner was one of the most enjoyable things she'd done in a long time. James had never enjoyed her food very much, always claiming that carbs weren't his thing.

The man had spent more time at the gym than doing anything else, which should have been a warning sign from the start.

Beau, even though he appeared to spend plenty of time lifting, was enjoying the meal like a starved man. Like her brother often ate when he enjoyed his meals.

"What?" he asked her, his eyes narrowing slightly. "Have I got sauce on my face?" He reached up and wiped his chin and she laughed again.

"If you didn't, you wouldn't be enjoying the food. Or so my mother often told my brother." She replied with a shrug.

"Your family." He set his fork down as he reached for another slice of bread. "They're all overweight, right?"

She laughed again. "No, we run a very busy restaurant. My mother is skinny, too skinny." She frowned remembering how her mother had looked the last time she'd seen her. "My dad and brother often try to outlift each other in the garage, where my dad built a home gym."

"I'm thinking of turning my garage into a home gym since I don't have a car," he answered between bites.

"You don't own a car?" she asked with a frown.

"Why would I? The store is less than a mile away. Anywhere I need to go, I can take *Ho'omau*. The hardware store delivers, as do most places on the island."

"I suppose..." She shook her head and realized how stupid it was to be freaked out. After all, a man who lives on a small island would have no real use for a car. "You're right. You live on an island. It's not like you're going to take a cross-country trip." She chuckled. "The boat was a smart move. You can island hop if you have to."

"I do all the time. Sometimes I even ferry friends between the islands just for fun." He chuckled. "Or a case of beer."

She smiled, not wanting to upset the easy conversation by mentioning his obvious dark past. Still, the journalist in her was dying to know what had happened to him that caused the lost look to consume him at any given moment.

"It's nice, having so many friends," she replied and the lost look was back behind his eyes. Okay, so it was obvious he'd lost friends. She knew from her experience of inter-viewing military personnel who had lost team members that it was equal to losing family.

"You wanted to know what happened," Beau said after setting his fork down again. "I lost my entire team." Then he nudged his empty plate away. "They were two of my brothers and my sister, Kim." He sighed heavily. "I was the only one left because I had paused to pick a desert flower." He looked down at his hands.

Nicky felt her heart kick in her chest. Still, her programming to know more had her asking, "How long ago?"

His eyes moved up to hers. "Two years, but I relive it every single moment. The sounds, the smells." He shook his head. "When I feel the vibration of a motor." He looked back down at his hands. "They were my lifeline. My *ohana*." He stood up and walked over to look out over the dark water.

"It matters." She followed him and lay a hand on his shoulder. "Their stories will live on in you," she said as he turned towards her.

His eyes narrowed and then he smiled. "I like that thought." He nodded, then brushed a strand of her hair away from her face. "I'd like to kiss you."

She smiled. "I'd like that, too," she said as he moved closer. When their lips met, she melted into him. Her knees, which had been perfectly solid moments ago, turned to liquid.

His arms wrapped around her, stopping her from melting completely as his mouth slanted over hers, gently nibbling her bottom lip.

"Beau," she sighed when he pulled back. Should she tell him that that was by far the best kiss she'd ever had? Somehow, his simple touch had rocked her deeper than any other. How? Why had it affected her so much?

Instead, she looked into his dark brown eyes and felt tears building behind her own eyes.

"Was it that bad?" he asked, with a slight smile.

She laughed. "My god." She covered her mouth with her hands. "Either I'm drunk off the one and a half glasses of wine or..."

"That was an amazing kiss," he finished with a smile.

She laughed and nodded. "Okay, not drunk."

"Maybe we both are?" he asked, pulling her into his arms. "I'd like you to stay, but somehow, it doesn't feel right. Not tonight," he said with a sigh.

She knew what he was saying. Agreed down in her gut. Still, if he'd asked her, she would have stayed. That weakness somehow made it more imperative to her that she head back to her bungalow.

"I'll walk you back," he said, taking her hand.

"You promised me dessert," she said, stopping him.

He chuckled and nodded. "Okay, fair enough. We'll eat it out on the deck, though, in the fresh air."

They ate chocolate eclairs out on the back deck of the boat, looking over the dock and the beach beyond. They could hear music from the resort's bar area. The soft sound floated on the wind, making everything feel romantic, including the twinkling lights that lit up the pathways.

"I can see why you like this place so much. You could totally forget that there is a busy world out there. People running the rat race, trampling over one another to get to the proverbial cheese. It's all so..."

"Exhausting," he finished for her. "It's why I came back here. Most of my childhood was spent on the beach." He smiled and looked out over the water. "Mateo, Kailani, and I spent most of our youth doing odd jobs around the resort to earn spending money. Kailani fell in love with Matt, the resort owner's son, at a very young age. When Matt's father died, he took over the resort. The first thing he did was marry Kailani, something his father had forbidden."

"Why?" Nicky asked with a frown.

"Because she didn't come from money. The fact that Kailani still chooses to work each day would have totally pissed the old man off," Beau said with a chuckle. "Matt, being Matt, loves it. Sometimes he even comes down and lends a hand." He was silent for a moment, then busted out laughing. "A few weeks back, he was working the booth when a customer complained and asked to see his supervisor. He had Kailani come over and talk to the woman."

Nicky was smiling. "They sound like a perfect couple."

"They are. Their son, Nohea, is my godson." He smiled. "He's two years old and more than a handful," he added as he finished his dessert. She'd finished a while back since he was doing most of the talking. "Shall we head out?" He motioned towards the beach.

"Sure." She dusted off her hands and grabbed her bag. He helped her off the boat and held her hand as they strolled down the dock.

"How are you liking your new digs?" he asked as they turned down the pathway beside the large pool. There were couples sitting around the water, enjoying the band that was playing on the stage beside the bar.

"I slept so peacefully last night with the sound of the ocean. Thank you, again, for arranging it."

He shrugged. "The least I could do. Especially after seeing what you have to deal with." He stopped walking on the pathway and turned to her. "Is he always like that?"

She thought about it for a moment. "When I first started working at SWE, he was extremely nice. Until I turned down his advances at the first Christmas party. He was there with his wife, who was sitting on Santa's lap, flirting. I think they're swingers. I mean, I don't think his wife, Jennifer, knows he's here with the blonde. But, then again, I'm not really sure she would care."

"I'm not the jealous type, but that's pushing the limits," he said easily.

"Agreed." She nodded as she thought about watching

Beau kissing anyone else. "Not something I'd sign up for either."

He nodded, then started walking again. "So, we agree then, while we're enjoying one another"—he glanced sideways at her and smiled— "we're exclusive."

She chuckled and then tugged on his hand to stop him again so she could wrap her arms around him. Lifting on her toes, she brushed her lips over his. "I like the way you negotiate."

His hands moved to her hips, and he balled her skirt in his fingers. Her fingers tangled in his hair, holding him close.

"I like that we both end up winning," he joked, and then he kissed her again.

When they pulled apart again, she was breathless and a little shaky. "I think I need my bed now." She rested her head against his chest.

"There's definitely something here," he said with his own sigh. "Get some rest." He dropped his hands, and she swayed slightly. "I'll see you again in the morning."

He took a step back and then turned and disappeared down the pathway.

She was smiling and practically floating on the air the rest of the way to her bungalow. Until she saw the dark shadow waiting outside her door.

"What are you doing here?" she asked Jake as she took out her key to unlock the door.

"We need to talk," he said firmly.

"It can wait until our morning meeting." She stepped inside with every intention of closing the door with him outside, but he put his hand on the door and pushed it opened.

"Now," he said, stepping past her.

She rolled her eyes, turned on the lights inside, and tossed down her bag. He stopped and looked around, then turned on her.

"How did you get this room?" he asked, his eyes narrowed.

"I asked for an upgrade." She crossed her arms over her chest. "Now that that is cleared up." She motioned to the door.

Jake strolled over to the window and stood there, looking out into the darkness.

"My contact is MIA," he said after a moment.

"Okay," she said slowly, knowing full well that he'd continue.

"I went to his place this afternoon. It was trashed." He turned to her. "There was blood."

"Did you call the police?" she asked.

"No." He shook his head. "For now, there's nothing to report. The authorities might think I had something—" He cut himself off. "No. For now, we'll continue to go off the information he provided. I'll send you the rest of what he sent me, so there's a backup." He pulled out his phone.

For the first time, Jake was starting to scare her. The man never shared information. With anyone.

Her phone chimed, signaling that she'd received the information. She wanted to look at it, but instead waited and watched Jake.

"I think we're all being watched," he added, putting his phone away and slightly nodding towards the glass doors. "I'd keep your curtains closed from here on out. We can't trust anyone outside of our tight circle." He walked towards the door. He stopped and glanced back towards her, his hand on the doorknob. "I'd be careful what you say around the boat captain, if I were you," he added before leaving.

CHAPTER NINE

Beau could tell something was different with Nicky that following morning. The entire trip out to the dive spot, she remained below with Leo and Gordy. As agreed, Jake was not on board.

Nicky had said less than two words to him that morning before they had left. He could see the worry in her eyes and wondered what had changed since the night before.

He didn't get a chance to talk to her alone before the four of them jumped into the water. Today, he was training Nicky and Gordy how to safely swim in the coral. They had discussed briefly going back to the cave, but Jake had been adamant that no one else know about the area, and Beau was not going to go in alone. No one else was trained yet.

While the four of them headed towards the reef, he talked about how the currents could change, what kind of emergencies usually arise, and what to do in those situations.

Leo messed with his camera equipment while the three of them ducked into the coral together. He picked a narrow spot and had each of them swim through it. Once they had done that a few times, he had them try again, this time sharing their reserve oxygen instead of using the full-face masks.

Nicky was a pro, but Gordy had a moment of panic once his mask was removed. Since he could no longer communicate with the headset in the full-face masks, he calmed the man down with hand signals until he and Nicky were easily passing the oxygen between each other.

He watched them carefully as they swam through the narrow passage. Again, Gordy froze for a split second since he had to follow behind Nicky and couldn't reach the oxygen. Beau was there, calming him down and getting him the mouthpiece again.

When they surfaced, Gordy looked exhausted, while Nicky looked excited and pumped.

"How are you doing?" he asked Gordy.

The man shook his head. "I'm not sure I'm built for it," he admitted.

"It takes practice and trust in your partner." He eyes moved to Nicky's. She quickly glanced away from him.

"Right." Gordy sighed. "I'm not sure I'm up for another try after lunch."

"No," Beau agreed. "I think that's all we should do for today."

"How about we use those?" Gordy suggested, motioning to the fishing poles he had for guests. "I'm pretty sure Jake is going to be upset if we come back early."

He glanced towards Nicky and Leo, who both shrugged.

"I could use some time to stare at the water," Leo answered. "Nicky?"

"Sure," she said as she put her equipment away.

"I've got some bait," Beau said, motioning to the live well. "We can catch some more with the nets."

"It's been years since I fished," Leo said, rubbing his hands together. "Care for a friendly wager?" he asked Gordy.

Beau watched as Nicky pulled on a pair of shorts and a flowing top before heading inside.

"Help yourselves," he told the men, and then he followed her inside.

She was sitting at the table, typing something on a laptop.

"Work?" he asked, walking over to grab a glass of water.

She glanced up. "Yes." She returned to looking at her screen.

"Problems?" he asked when she frowned at the screen.

"Possibly. How well do you know Tomas Rubio?"

"Tomas..." He frowned as he shook his head. "The name isn't familiar."

"Do you know him now?" she asked, motioning to her screen. He looked down at the image on the screen. It was a social media photo of a man in his mid-twenties. The man looked a little familiar, but Beau didn't pay that much attention to everyone he took out on the water.

"Possibly." He sat down next to her and looked a little closer.

Before he had a chance, however, she scrolled the screen and a different image of the sandy-blond man appeared. This time he was smiling as he held up a large fish. The picture had clearly been taken on the *Ho'omau*, and he could even see himself in the background, talking to another person, who was just off screen.

"Well, that clears that up. I guess I've taken the guy out fishing before," he said easily.

"There's more than just this one," Nicky said, scrolling. Several more images of the man on Beau's boat appeared. They were clearly from different days since the guy's clothing had changed. "From the looks of it, you've taken him out several times. So, again, I'll ask, how well do you know Tomas Rubio?"

Beau frowned. Who was Tomas Rubio? Why would Nicky be upset that he knew him?

Beau shook his head. "I don't know him. It appears that I've taken him out on a charter, as I do hundreds of people each year. Why? Why is he important?"

"This, apparently, is Jake's contact. Who has disappeared." She turned the screen back to herself. "His last post was the day before we arrived."

"He's a local?" Beau asked, frowning.

Nicky's eyes moved to his as she slowly nodded.

He could see it behind those eyes. The distrust. Now he knew what was bothering Nicky.

"It's a small island, but that doesn't mean I know everyone," he said. Then he glanced out where Leo was cheering as he reeled in a catch. "Come with me, after I drop them off." He motioned to the two outside.

"Where?" she asked, her eyes narrowing.

"You're obviously questioning if you can trust me." He took her hand in his. "Let me show you that you can." He saw her expression change.

She nodded slowly as an answer, and he smiled. "Good, now, let's head out and catch some fish."

Over the next hour, the four of them caught more than half a dozen fish each. When the live well was full, they headed back to shore.

"I'll pick you up at five," he told Nicky as he helped her onto the dock.

She nodded. "What should I wear?"

He looked down at her shorts and T-shirt and shrugged. "What you're wearing is fine."

She frowned down at her clothes. "Casual it is." She threw her bag over her shoulder and left.

He sent out more than a dozen text messages and then spent the next hour cleaning all of the fish they'd caught earlier. Once done, he showered, pulled on a pair of fresh board shorts and a button-up shirt, and headed out to get Nicky.

She too had changed from the shorts and top she'd worn all day. Now she was wearing a pair of white capri pants and a flowing soft pink blouse.

"You look nice." He leaned in and placed a kiss on her cheek. The fact that she didn't tense at his touch was a good sign.

"Thanks," she said, tossing her bag over her shoulder and then shutting her door. "Shall we?" She motioned and he took her hand and started walking down the pathway, back towards the docks.

"It's a little bit of trip," he explained.

"I have no plans. Jake sent a text and called off our meeting for tonight. He said something about not feeling well." She rolled her eyes.

He helped her climb aboard the *Ho'omau* again and within five minutes, they were heading out into open water.

"So, where are we heading to?" she asked, sitting beside him.

He glanced over at her. "Molokai."

"Okay," she said slowly, settling back for the fifteen-minute trip.

When they came close to shore, he cut the engines and let the boat coast a little closer to the sandy shores. There were already several other smaller boats anchored closer to the beach.

"How are we going to get to shore?" she asked, frowning at him.

"*Hau'oli*, the dinghy." He motioned to the small boat that sat directly in front of them. "It means happy." He dropped anchor, stopping their forward motion. "Come on, you can help me load the coolers."

It wasn't difficult to swing the small boat over the railing, as it was on a winch system. After they loaded the two massive coolers full of the fish they'd caught, which he'd cleaned on board, he dropped the boat into the water and helped Nicky climb down the ladder.

"Is there a party?" she asked, motioning to the beach, where he could see the fire already going as everyone gathered around.

"I called my *'ohana*," he said with a shrug. "Character references." He smiled.

Nicky's eyes narrowed. "You're idea of getting me to trust you is to introduce me to your family?"

He nodded and started the small engine. The *Hau'oli* jetted towards the sand.

The private locals-only beach was one of the best on all of the islands. Barely any tourists had stepped foot on it, which was one of the reasons it was the best.

He remembered the parties they had attended there when he was a kid. Most of them had hundreds of locals and usually included several full-sized roasted pigs.

Because of the short notice, his fish, along with whatever everyone else brought along, would suffice. Punahele, Kailani's cousin, met them at the beach and helped him pull the dinghy further up into the sand next to the other boats.

"Aloha." Pun smiled at him and wrapped his beefy arms around him. "I see you brought a friend."

"Aloha. Nicky"—he turned to her and took her hand—"this is Punahele, or Pun for short."

"Aloha," Nicky said and then laughed when Pun gave her a bear hug.

"Welcome. Come, the roast has started." Pun took one of the coolers and Beau grabbed the other.

"Go on," Beau said, motioning. "You remember Kailani." He nodded towards the group where his friend stood holding her wiggly son, Nohea. Both mother and son were laughing.

As he looked around the beach, he smiled at all of the family that had come out at such a short notice.

He followed Pun to a large table where a few others were seasoning and wrapping other fish in banana leaves. After dropping off the fish, he was handed a beer and slowly made his way over to where Kailani was introducing Nicky to everyone. Matt now had their son and was chasing him around the sand, along with the kids of several other of his friends.

"Hey," he said to Nicky as he handed her a cold beer. "I hope beer is okay?"

She smiled. "Thanks. Kailani was introducing me to everyone." She took a deep breath. "I'll be lucky to remember any of their names."

Kailani laughed. "If you can't remember someone's name, sistah or braddah works."

"Good to know." Nicky smiled as she took a sip of her beer. She glanced down at the label. "This is good."

"Kani and Kini brew it themselves," Beau said, motioning to the thirty-year-old twins, who ran their own brewery.

"We sell it at the resort," Kailani added. "Along with Apona's breads and desserts, and meats, eggs, and vegetables from the Māhoe family's farm." She motioned with her own beer to each of the people as she continued. "'*Ohana* takes care of '*ohana*," she finished with a smile.

"I like that. It obviously pays off. I mean, your resort is top notch and hands down the best I've been to," Nicky said easily.

"I'll make sure my husband knows," Kailani said. "Now, what do you say we head over and help get things ready for the feast?" She took Nicky's arm and started across the sand, then she glanced over at him. "Shouldn't you be lending a hand too?" She nodded to where he'd dropped off the fish.

Sighing, he nodded and disappeared to help out. He knew it was Kailani's way of saying she wanted time alone with Nicky. After all, Nicky was the first person he'd brought to one of the family gatherings. The first one he had called his family together for.

As he helped prep the food, he wondered why it mattered so much what Nicky thought of him. He didn't want her to believe he had anything to do with the treasure or her boss's contact disappearing. Hell, he'd told the truth. He didn't know who Tomas Rubio was. He didn't remember the guy at all from the pictures.

At some of the busiest times, he could easily take out more than a dozen fishing charters a week. If Tomas was a local, he wasn't one that ran in Beau's circles.

Still, that thought gave him an idea, and he started asking everyone around him if they knew the guy. It wasn't until he asked his friend Doni as they helped cart some ice to the drinks area that he finally got some information.

"Tomas?" she said with a frown. "Sure, why are you asking?"

He pulled Doni aside. "Is he reliable?"

She thought about it for a moment. "As far as I know. He's only been on the island for..."—she thought, tilting her head— "less than a year. He comes into the mart at least twice a week." She frowned. "I haven't seen him this week at all."

Doni worked down at the local grocery mart. If Beau had been thinking clearly, he would have asked her first since she knew everyone on the island. He wasn't joking, either. Every local at one point walked through Doni's doors.

"Reliable enough," she added. "Why?"

Beau nodded towards Nicky, who appeared to be having a great time with his friends. She was sitting around the fire, drinking her second beer, talking with Alana and a few others.

"Nicky's boss heard something from the guy and then Tomas up and disappeared on him when it came time to meet. Any idea why the guy would bail?" he asked.

Doni frowned. "No, as I mentioned, I haven't seen him all week. Come to think of it, the last time he was in, he looked... off."

"Off? How so?"

"He had a few bruises and a bloody lip. He claimed he'd fallen off a ladder, but..." She shrugged. "He was looking around, nervous-like."

Beau glanced over as he heard Nicky laughing. "Come with me." He took Doni's hand. "I need you to tell Nicky what you just told me."

"Sure," she said, laughing and struggling to keep up

with him. "God, you're all legs," she joked, and he slowed down for the shorter woman.

"Nicky, this is Doni. She owns and runs the local grocery mart." He waited a heartbeat. "She knows Tomas Rubio."

He watched Nicky's eyebrows shoot up. "You do?" she asked Doni.

"Sure, I know all the locals on the island. Not that most would consider Tomas a local. He's been here less than a year," Doni said with a shrug.

Nicky's eyes moved to his. He could tell what she wanted to ask Doni, and could see she didn't want to ask with him standing right there. "I'll leave you two..." He stormed off. It hurt, knowing that Nicky thought he'd lied to her about knowing the guy. Still, if Doni knew something about Tomas that could help, then he'd done the right thing.

"What put you in such a bad mood, brah?" Matt said, walking over and slapping him on the shoulder.

"Nothing," he instantly denied.

Matt laughed. "Right." Matt's eyes moved to where Nicky was talking with Doni. "I remember that feeling myself not so long ago."

"What feeling?" Beau asked him, causing Matt to laugh again.

"You'll figure it out. For now, how about we hit the surf?" He motioned to a couple of long boards sitting in the sand. "You can paddle off all that frustration," Matt suggested.

"Sure." He followed Matt, tossing off his shirt. He grabbed a board and let the waves wash away his feelings.

CHAPTER TEN

Nicky didn't know why Beau was upset, but it was obvious he was when he left her alone with Doni.

"Not sure why you want to know about Tomas, but Beau seemed to think it was important enough to drag me across the sand." Doni laughed and sipped her beer.

"Do you really know Tomas?" she asked, turning her attention away from Beau.

"Sure do. Like I told Beau, the guy comes into the mart twice a week," Doni answered.

"When was the last time you saw him?" Nicky asked.

Doni thought about it. "It must have been about a week ago. His face was covered in bruises, and he had a fat lip. I told Beau that Tomas claimed he'd fallen off a ladder, but..." She shook her head. "The man looked scared."

"Scared?" Nicky asked.

"Yes. He kept looking over his shoulder. I've seen a few women look like that. Ones whose husbands beat them." Doni shook her head.

Nicky's eyes moved over to watch Beau toss his shirt in the sand and pick up the longest surfboard she'd ever seen.

For a moment, she was mesmerized, watching him carry the heavy thing into the water. Then she watched each stroke as he glided effortlessly through the waves.

"You've got it bad," Doni said, breaking into Nicky's assessment of Beau.

"Hm?" She tore her attention from the sexy man and back to the shorter middle-aged woman. Doni laughed at her.

"So, why does your boss need to talk to Tomas?" Doni asked.

Instead of answering, Nicky asked, "Does Beau know Tomas?"

Doni frowned. "Doubt it, considering the way he asked about the guy. Besides, they don't run in the same circles."

"Okay, so..." She pulled out her phone and showed Doni the image of Tomas and Beau.

Doni laughed. "I doubt Beau remembers half the people he takes out. The only reason I remember anyone is that I see them over and over. Locals, that is. Forget about the tourists. I wouldn't remember you if you walked in my mart tomorrow. That is, if I hadn't met you here," she added with a wink.

"Okay." Nicky tucked her phone back into her bag. She felt like a heel. Beau had been telling the truth, and she'd questioned him.

"For what it's worth, Beau is one of the most honest and charming men I've ever met. It's hard, knowing what he went through a few years back. He returned to the islands broken. Working with Kailani has helped. That and working on that house of his." Doni laughed. "Idle minds and all that. It's been good for him."

Nicky nodded, not knowing what else to say. Then Doni touched her arm. "Something tells me you matter to him." She motioned to the water where Beau was riding a wave in. "You wouldn't be here, if you didn't." She motioned around. "Whether you know it or not, now you're *'ohana.*" She chuckled and turned to walk away.

Nicky thought about that as she walked through the sand to the edge of the water. She slipped off her sandals and walked ankle deep into the water to watch Beau and Matt enjoying themselves. Moments later, they were joined by several other people.

Punahele grabbed her hand and pulled her to a long board. She tossed off her shorts and top, leaving her in the two-piece striped swimsuit she wore underneath. She sat on the front of the board as Pun paddled her out into the water, straight for Beau, who was sitting on the board, watching them.

"I found your woman," Pun said to Beau, causing him to laugh.

"She's not mine. But I'll take her," Beau joked. He then pulled up beside them and lifted her directly off the board and onto his.

"Having fun?" he asked after Pun paddled out further.

"So far," she nodded. "Thanks."

"Did you find out what you needed?" he asked after a moment.

She glanced over her shoulder at him and nodded. "Thanks."

The hurt and anger that had been behind his eyes earlier were gone, replaced with laughter and joy. So much that she couldn't help but feel the emotions herself.

"For?" he asked her.

"Making the connections." She motioned around them. "For introducing me to your family," she added with a smile. "I think they like me."

He laughed. "They have great taste. Want to catch a wave?" he asked.

"I..." She felt her stomach clench. "I've never surfed."

He laughed again. "All you have to do is hang on."

She nodded and then felt him shift under her. Soon, the board was turned around as he paddled them further out to where everyone else was lined up, waiting for a wave.

"When I say so, stand up with me," Beau told her as he began paddling faster. She felt the moment the board was swept up with the wave, felt the shift as Beau started to stand. "Now," he said, and she felt his hands on her hips, guiding her to stand.

She laughed as he took her hips, turning her slightly and helping her correct her stance. "See, nothing to it," he said when the wave died down. "Now we sit." He helped her back down. "And do it all over again."

On their fifth trip, she shifted and fell off balance, forcing them both into the water. Still, Beau came up laughing and holding onto her.

"Are you okay?" he asked as he helped her back onto the board. It was harder than getting on one in the shallow water.

"Yes," she laughed, pushing her hair out of her face. "That was my fault."

"Taking a dip is never anyone's fault. It's a joy," he said, climbing on board behind her. "Remember that," he added. "How about we head in for some food?"

"I could eat." She helped him paddle them to shore.

They sat in the sand, eating poke, which consisted of grilled fish, rice, seaweed, avocados, and a creamy sauce. It was so delicious, she went back for seconds when Beau did. There was fresh pineapple and even grilled pineapple for dessert.

As the sun set, someone pulled out a ukulele and, to her surprise, handed it to Beau, who started strumming along with Pun as everyone gathered around the fire. She was handed another beer and sat back to enjoy the music with the rest.

At some point, people started gathering their things, piling them into their boats, and heading off into the darkness.

She helped Beau return his two empty coolers to the dinghy, and they said their goodbyes.

"You're just full of surprises," she said as they headed back to his boat. Thanks to a full moon in the night sky, she could see him perfectly. He looked even better bathed in moonlight.

"Hm?" he asked, glancing over at her.

"You play ukulele and surf like a pro. Not to mention, you have a pretty good singing voice." She nudged his knees with her own.

He chuckled and reached up to brush her hair away from her face. "You're not such a bad surfer yourself."

"Thanks to you," she responded as they came up to his boat. She helped him get the dinghy back in place, which was easier than she'd thought it would be.

They sat in the captain's chairs as they made their way across the dark water towards the lights of Maui. The resort was the brightest spot in the distance.

"Did you know that the entire crew was drunk when the *Pride of Hawaii*, the ship that carried the Hawaiian king's treasure, sank?" He glanced over at her with a smile.

"No." She shook her head. "Seriously?"

"The treasure was lost for over a hundred years," Beau added. "Lokelani's treasure has been missing for almost double that. Do you really think Tomas knows where it's at?"

Nicky had been thinking about that since she'd talked with Doni. From what the woman had said about the man, there wasn't anything out of the ordinary about him.

Nicky seriously doubted that he owned his own boat, since he'd chartered Beau's a few times. So if he'd found the treasure diving, he would have had to have someone take him out and possibly even witness the find.

So why would Tomas drag Jake all the way out there for a story? How did Jake know Tomas? More and more questions swirled in her head as they docked, and Beau cut the engines. One thing was now perfectly clear to her—the evening had done what Beau had wanted it to, she no longer distrusted him.

"Did you have fun?" Beau asked, turning in his chair and looking at her.

"I did." She nodded. "I like your family."

He smiled. "They liked you. Several of them made a point to mention that I should bring you for our next gathering."

"I'd like that. If I'm still around," she added. His smile slipped a little.

"I'll walk you back to your place," he suggested. She nodded but before he could stand up, she leaned over and placed her lips over his. "What was that for?" he asked with a smile.

"That was an apology. For not trusting you."

He chuckled. "I don't blame you. We've only known each other a few days. It's unreasonable to assume you'd trust me over pictures."

She sighed, then leaned in and kissed him again.

"What was that one for?" he asked, his hands going to her hips.

"Because I liked the first one and wanted to do it again," she admitted, causing him to laugh.

"I like that reason a lot more than the first one."

He took her hand, and as they strolled towards her bungalow, they talked about his friends and family. About the gossip they'd overheard or about what the following day would hold.

When they turned onto the pathway that led to her bungalow, she gasped when she noticed the door was wide open. She felt Beau tense, then shove her behind him.

"Stay here," he said quietly.

Before she had time to argue, he disappeared inside the dark room.

She fumbled to pull her phone out of her bag, but before she had a chance to call someone for help, a figure appeared in the doorway. She screamed as a man dressed in all black pushed past her, knocking into her and sending her sprawling onto the ground.

Before she had time to recover, hands were grabbing her, and she screamed again.

"Easy, it's me," Beau said, wrapping his arms around her. "Are you okay?" he asked, concerned.

"I..." She mentally assessed herself. "I'm okay," she finished as he helped her stand up. "You?"

Instead of answering, he turned away from her, looking into the bungalow. "He trashed the place." He motioned and she noticed that the lights were on inside now. "I'm going to call the front desk and let them know what's happened. They'll call the police." He walked back inside and picked up the phone from the table by the bed.

She stepped inside and gasped at the destruction inside.

It wasn't until he hung up that she noticed that his lip was bleeding.

"You've been hit!" She gasped and rushed to the bathroom. She wet a towel and then returned to his side and dabbed his lip dry.

"He sucker punched me when I turned on the light." Beau shrugged. "I'm okay." Just then two staff members rushed up the walkway.

Nicky stood back as Beau explained what had happened. She overheard him informing them that a new room wouldn't be necessary for her since she would be staying with him, and she was too tired to argue.

Besides, she didn't want to be left alone tonight. The thought of spending the night with Beau warded off the chill that had consumed her from the moment she'd found the door to her place open.

CHAPTER ELEVEN

Nicky was behaving like a zombie. He could tell that she was at the end of her energy level because she allowed him to steer her and direct her so easily.

Normally, he wouldn't have taken the reins, but when she didn't argue about staying with him on the boat, he figured she was too tired to say anything.

"You can have this room," he said, setting her bags down inside the guest room, the only other cabin that had a queen-size bed. "The bathroom is across the hall," he said as she moved into the room and looked around.

"This is nice, but I was hoping..." She turned to him, wrapped her arms around his shoulders, and kissed him.

Instantly, his body reacted. There was no doubt that he wanted her. Had wanted her since the moment he'd seen her standing across the sand.

She pulled him backwards until his legs bumped into the bed, then she nudged him and had them falling onto the mattress. She laughed as she landed on top of him. Her hands roamed over his chest, moved up his neck, and buried into his hair as her mouth kept sliding over his.

"Nicky," he groaned when she nudged his shirt off.

"Just let me," she moaned, pulling the shirt over his head.

Seeing the determination in her eyes, he knew that she was acting on desperation and desire. Much like himself. Without thinking, he pulled her shirt and shorts off. He paused and took some time to appreciate her toned legs. He ran his hands up and down them, enjoying the two-piece swimsuit she wore, the only remaining piece of clothing on her.

"Beau." His name was a whisper before she tugged him back down to her and their lips connected once more. He wanted to move fast, to enjoy the taste, the feeling of her underneath him, but at the same time, he knew that in order for them to fully enjoy it, they needed to slow down. A lot.

When she reached for the hem of his boardshorts, he pulled back, just out of her reach. He ran his eyes over her and smiled down at her when she frowned back up at him.

"Don't pout." He ran a finger down between her breasts and saw her eyes fill with heat. Leaning down, he ran his tongue over the same pathway, taking a moment to pull the material away from her heated skin and take her left nipple into his mouth. Her fingers dug into his hair as she slowly moved underneath him, wrapping her legs around his legs.

He moved lower, tracing her ribs, around her belly button, then slid the bottoms of her suit off her legs. He trailed his tongue across her pussy and nudged her legs wide so he could settle there and enjoy tasting her, pleasing her.

The sexy sounds she made as he slid his finger and tongue in and out of her were almost enough to make him lose his hold. He didn't move up until he tasted her release on his tongue, heard her cry out his name, felt her convulse around him.

But as he slid up her body, he quickly realized that she was moments away from falling asleep. Smiling, he pulled her into his arms instead.

"Hmm, I want..." she said, her words slurred.

"Tomorrow," he said. He held her until her breathing leveled and his own body cooled off.

He woke to the sound of a boat horn. He jerked awake like he did when he'd had the dream filled with twisted memories. But after a moment, he realized he'd slept through the entire night peacefully. No nightmares.

His arms were wrapped around a soft, warm woman, who appeared to be nibbling on his neck and ear.

Smiling, he remembered pleasing Nicky the night before, and his body was instantly fully awake.

"Morning," she purred against his skin. "I think I owe you breakfast."

He chuckled and she laughed when he rolled over to pin her underneath him.

"I'll have mine in bed," he said before he kissed her and settled between her legs.

Unlike the night before, this morning there was a great urgency boiling. In the back of his mind, he knew that her coworkers would be there soon. He wanted to prolong their time together but needed her more than he had last night.

"Beau, I need you now," she said against his ear.

Reaching out, he opened the nightstand drawer and then cursed when he realized he wasn't in his normal cabin.

"Here," Nicky said, leaning over to grab her bag. She returned with a condom.

"Thanks," he said and then kissed her again, needing to hurry even more.

When he slid into her, he felt something deep inside him shift, something that had been missing in his life up until that very moment. He forced himself to push it aside, to enjoy the moment, enjoy being with her.

Her legs wrapped around his hips, holding him deep inside her. When they moved together, it was as if he was experiencing something brand new, something so over-whelming that he no longer cared about time or place. Then he felt her tighten around him, heard her cry of release, and knew that no power in the universe could stop his own.

"That was..." Nicky started, her arms wrapped around his middle. Her legs had fallen slightly but were still wrapped around him. "Wow."

He smiled into her hair and nodded. "Yeah, wow." He sighed.

"I don't want to move but..." She took a deep breath.

"Leo and Gordy will be here soon," he finished. He felt her nod.

"Shower, I'll go make us some breakfast." Before he got up, he kissed her again. "God, you taste so good."

She smiled up at him. "You're just saying that because you're hungry."

He chuckled. "I'm saying that because you taste like honey," he corrected. "I'll want more later." He quickly got up before he could decide to stay there in bed with her for the rest of the day.

Detouring to the back, he jumped into the water off the port side to cool off and to clear his head before heading into the kitchen to make scrambled eggs and bacon and to dice up some fresh fruit.

By the time Nicky appeared, Leo and Gordy were already on board, enjoying the breakfast they had brought along. Since Nicky had come from the back, no one had noticed that she'd already been on board.

The day proceeded much like the one before. He spent a few hours teaching Nicky and Gordy how to handle situations that could come up while cave diving or reef diving.

Gordy seemed more relaxed today than he'd been the day before and, after a short lunch break, they spent another couple of hours working while Leo took pictures and video. The man seemed to really be into nature filming and even talked about getting into it full time after his retirement.

After seeing some of the pictures he'd taken that day, he had to admit, the man was good.

By the time they docked, Nicky had told both Leo and Gordy about the break-in and that she was staying on the boat with Beau in the guest cabin. They both seemed concerned that someone had broken into her place, but Leo suggested that the bungalows were a hot spot for thieves since they sat off the beaten path.

Neither of them cared that Nicky was staying on the boat or with him. Instead, they were more concerned about being attacked themselves by whoever had broken in.

"Are you sure you're okay?" Leo asked Nicky as they were getting ready to leave for the evening.

"I am." Nicky smiled. "Beau is here and, as he mentioned, there's security around the clock at the docks."

"Good." Leo nodded. "We'll see you at the dinner meeting."

Beau heard Nicky groan as Leo left.

"Dinner meeting?" he asked her once they were alone.

"Jake." She rolled her eyes. "I think it's his way of controlling things since he can't do it from onboard any longer."

"Right." He nodded. "We can shower and head up

together. I don't really feel like cooking dinner for myself tonight."

Nicky's smile brightened. "I'd like that."

After refueling and making sure the *Ho'omau* was secure, they headed downstairs to his larger room and showered.

Just being able to run his hands over Nicky again solidified the immenseness of his desire for her, which he'd felt all day long. Even though his shower was in no way designed for two bodies, they found a way to move together, more slowly than that morning.

When he grew frustrated about the lack of space, he shut the water off and carried her into the bed.

An hour later, they arrived at the dining hall late for her appointment. He had asked her if she wanted to walk in by herself and let him come in later so she wouldn't get any grief from Jake, but she pushed her chin up and grabbed his hand instead.

"My personal life is no concern of his or my employer. Besides," she added with a smile, "I just know it's going to piss him off, and you know how I love to see that." She raised her eyebrows.

He laughed as they stepped inside, but his smile fell away when he noticed who was sitting at the table with Jake, Leo, and Gordy. His plan was to sit at the bar while they had their meeting, but instead, he followed her to the table and glared down at Glenn Palakiko.

The man was the lieutenant governor of Hawaii. He had one year of his four-year term left, and according to the polls, wasn't favored to get reelected. Mainly because he was a snake. He'd run on a family-values ticket and, months after he won, he divorced his wife of ten years and was spotted with several other women.

That hadn't even been the worst of it. There were rumors going around that Governor Kāne's health issues of the past year were being scrutinized. The older man had seemed in great health until an outing with Palakiko, when he'd taken a sudden turn.

But the main reason Beau didn't like the guy was the way he treated people he believed were below him.

"Evening," Beau said warmly, his eyes locking with Palakiko's. Beau noted that his instantly narrowed with irritation.

"Evening," Gordy and Leo replied warmly. Jake just narrowed his eyes slightly. Beau was positive it was due to Nicky's hand still locked in his.

"Mind if I join you?" he asked, not waiting for a response. He pulled out a chair for Nicky, then took a chair from another table behind them and pulled it in beside Nicky's spot.

"Glenn, I hadn't heard you were on the island," Beau said quickly.

Glenn's head tilted. "I wasn't aware my secretary had to check in with you each time I visit."

Beau chuckled as if it was an old joke.

"Do you two know each other?" Jake asked, and Beau wanted to roll his eyes.

"We're neighbors," Glenn supplied.

"Oh?" Jake looked at Beau. "I thought you lived on your boat?"

Beau laughed again. "Nope, just some of the time."

"I've been trying to purchase the *Wahi maluhia* since before Beau stole it out from under me," Glenn responded with a clipped tone.

"The *Wahi maluhia*?" Jake asked.

"It means peaceful spot. It's the name of the home that

sits directly between my new mansion and the water," Glenn said.

"*Wahi maluhia* means safe place," Jake corrected. "And that land had been in Kailani and Mateo's family for more generations than can be counted."

"And I can't help but wonder why they handed it over to you," Glenn added.

"Because Beau is their *'ohana*," Nicky chimed in. The moment her words hit him, he smiled, and he felt his entire body relax. Reaching over, he took her hand in his.

"Exactly." He felt even more warmth for her spread from his heart.

CHAPTER TWELVE

It was extremely obvious that Beau and Glenn didn't like one another. Jake tried his best to get Beau to leave the table, but Beau made it clear that as long as Glenn was there, he was staying put.

During the meal, the conversation was limited to a big storm that was brewing in the Pacific and heading their way. She knew Jake was upset about Beau being there, but she was thankful he'd stayed instead of heading to the bar to have dinner alone.

Already, she felt closer to Beau than she felt for anyone else at the table, and she had worked with Jake for several years.

Beau seemed more at ease the longer the dinner dragged on. When the table was cleared of dishes, Jake cleared his throat to get everyone's attention.

"Beau, I know you're chartering my crew off island each day, but this next part doesn't really concern you. We certainly don't want to keep you longer than we have to," he said clearly.

Beau smiled and looked towards Nicky for instruction.

She nodded and said, "I'll meet you at the bar and we can walk back to the docks together."

Beau nodded before saying his farewells and heading to the bar.

"Together?" Jake asked.

"Nicky's staying on the boat. Someone broke into her bungalow last night and trashed the place," Gordy supplied.

"Oh, how horrible," Jake said dryly, and Nicky felt a shiver race up her spine. "I guess there was a downside to staying in a bungalow."

"Right." She nodded, feeling her back teeth grind together.

There was a moment of silence and then Jake turned to Glenn. "You have the floor."

"Thank you." Glenn turned to them, his eyes landing on Nicky. "I believe that what your team is doing here is of interest to me. I've hired a professional team to take over for you."

At this point, Gordy jumped in, "This is our story."

Nicky felt her temper rise slightly but knew that there was probably nothing she could do to change Jake's mind. If he'd given up the story, there was little to nothing she could do.

"Oh, it's still your story," Glenn said with a smile. "Only you'll be telling it, not living it. The team I've hired is one of the best, and you'll be filming them the entire time. The story is yours. The treasure is mine." His eyes locked on Nicky.

The man hadn't taken his eyes off her the entire time he'd talked, and it was making her skin crawl.

Then Glenn turned to Jake and a look passed between them. It was obvious to her journalistic eyes that the men had a side bargain in play.

Nicky wondered what kind of deal the men had made and why. Why had Jake given up any information about the treasure hunt in the first place? True, her team was seriously under-skilled. Hell, she'd wondered from the start why he'd dragged them all the way to Hawaii. But then the pieces had started falling into place. The blonde, the lack of a real contact.

But pulling the lieutenant governor of Hawaii into the mix? Maybe this trip wasn't just a means for Jake to have an affair and a vacation. Maybe, just maybe, there was more to them being there?

As she strolled hand in hand with Beau across the beach towards the docks, she thought about everything that had happened since she'd arrived on the island.

About Jake's contact Tomas. What Doni had said about the man, which had been practically nothing.

"So, with the storm coming, all trips are cancelled for the day after tomorrow. I was thinking you'd like to come with me to my place?" Beau said when they got back to his boat, surprising her.

"Your place?" She switched gears in her mind. "Um, sure." She realized she hadn't even told him the news yet. She turned and looked up into his eyes as they stood on the docks. "Glenn Palakiko was there tonight because Jake has shared what he knows about the treasure with him. He's having a team take over starting tomorrow. We'll still be going out with them, but only to film what they find."

Beau was quiet for a moment. "I'm still taking your team out?" he asked. She nodded in response. "Okay," he said, taking her hand and helping her onto the deck of the boat.

"That's it? Just... okay?" she asked, feeling frustrated.

"Sure. I mean, you're an investigative journalist, not a professional treasure diver."

She crossed her arms over her chest. "I got the hint that you don't like Glenn tonight."

"I don't," he responded quickly. "He's a politician and a snake. Besides, you saw how he talked to the waitstaff."

She had noticed how the man treated the waitress as if she were nothing more than a nuisance. She knew that Beau knew each and every one of them and probably considered them to be family as well.

"Yeah," she sighed. "I know we're not treasure hunters, but... I didn't really believe there was anything to this." She motioned around them. "To why we were here. In my opinion, it was Jake's way of getting me out of the way for the promotion I was up for all while he got a paid vacation to be with his lover."

"Right."

"But now, bringing in a professional team and working with the local government..." She dropped off and noticed Beau thinking about it too.

"Let's shut it down for tonight." He pulled her into his arms. Her entire body melted against his. How was he able to do this to her? She'd had plenty of relationships before, but none had ever made her feel this wonderful this soon.

"What were you thinking?" she purred, running her hands over his arms and chest.

He leaned in and rubbed his lips over hers. She tasted the wine he'd had on the tip of his tongue, felt his hands on her narrow hips, pulling her close until she could feel the hardness of his erection against her stomach. She wanted him. More than she'd wanted him last night and this morning.

Just one taste of him and she was hooked.

"Dessert," he said once he pulled back. "I have some cheesecake..." he started, but she laughed and started pulling him inside.

She felt Beau tense before she saw the dark figure sitting on the sofa cushions.

"What the..." Beau jerked her behind him as he reached for a light switch. The moment the room was bathed in brightness, Nicky screamed.

There was so much blood. Too much of it. Instantly, she knew that whoever it was sitting there was gone. Had been gone for a long while, since his face was greyish white. Dark eyes stared directly at them as Beau cursed under his breath.

"Come on." He tried to pull her back outside, but her entire body was ice cold and frozen into place. Finally, with another curse, he lifted her into his arms and carried her outside into the warm night air and set her down on the bench. "Stay put. I'm calling the police."

She nodded and closed her eyes. But it didn't do any good. The image was seared onto her retinas, and she could still see the body clearly.

Then she gasped. "That is Tomas Rubio," she said to Beau, who nodded at her.

"Yeah, I know," he said, and then he started talking to the dispatcher.

Her eyes scanned the deck of the boat, the empty dock, as her mind whirled and tried to figure everything out. Had Tomas been killed on the boat? If not, how had they gotten his body here? Why here? Plus, where did all that blood come from? Thinking back, she played the scene over in her head, pushing the gore and the horror aside and letting her investigative mind see everything for what it was.

The blood didn't fit, no matter how she looked at it. She

would wager that the scene had been staged. She was sure the police investigation would prove her right. The blood did not come from Tomas.

She checked her watch and estimated that they'd only been gone an hour and forty minutes. Not enough time for Tomas to look like he did. Even with tons of blood loss, the man had obviously died hours if not days earlier.

So why had someone dumped him on Beau's boat? Why had they staged it to look as if he'd been killed there and recently? She stood up and started pacing, something she often did when she was trying to work out a puzzle.

When Beau reached up and stopped her, she realized he'd ended the call.

"Are you okay?" he asked her.

"Yes, I am now." She touched his shoulder. "It just... caught me off guard."

"Is this the first time you've seen... someone?"

"No. Still, it's not like I see them every day, but..." She shook her head. "I wasn't prepared."

"Are you now?"

She sighed. "Now I'm pissed. Someone is obviously trying to set you up for murder or..."

"Or?" he asked, waiting.

"Or sending you a message." She felt a shiver race through her.

"Right." He glanced towards the doors, then back out to the docks. "Where is Luano?" he asked, running his eyes over the dock before turning back to her. "We'd better go check on him, see what he knows before the police get here."

She nodded and followed him down the dock to the small security hut. Normally, when she'd pass by, there was a middle-aged man sitting behind the glass. The first time, she'd had to show her ID and sign in. Every time since, she'd just signed the sheet that sat in the window while the man had waved her through.

"Luano?" Beau called out as he opened the door to the hut. She turned away quickly this time when she saw the dark figure on the ground.

"He's alive," Beau said after rushing to the man's side. "Can you help?"

She rushed in and, after seeing the blood on the man's head, grabbed a T-shirt that was sitting on the back of a chair and held the material against the cut just above the man's left ear.

Beau got back on his phone, and she overheard him requesting an ambulance. Luano moaned slightly when she put more pressure on his cut.

"Easy," she said. "Help is on the way."

"Beau," the man moaned.

"He's here," she said and then watched the man flinch.

"No, he's the one who hit me," Luano said.

"What?" she and Beau said at the same time.

"That's not possible. He was with me," she said.

Luano shook his head and glanced past her straight up at Beau, then his eyes narrowed. "It was you," he said in an almost whisper.

"I've been in the dining room since we left the dock"— Beau glanced at his watch— "an hour and fifty minutes ago."

Luano closed his eyes. "All I know is, I saw you just before everything went dark."

Nicky turned to Beau. "You don't have some long-lost twin out there, do you?"

He shook his head as he frowned. "No."

"Okay, then someone is definitely setting you up.

Which means we'll have to do some quick explaining when the police arrive."

"Right," Beau said with a sigh.

She had wondered what a police station on one of the islands would look like and was seriously disappointed that it looked just like those she'd visited in the city while on a job. The only difference was the serious lack of hustle and bustle.

There were a few drunk tourists making some noise and a very angry passenger that had been pulled from a flight prior to departure. But there were no late-night partiers vomiting in the lobby and a serious lack of shouting, which was a positive.

They sat at the desk of an officer named Jay, whom Beau seemed to know. Jay asked them all the basic questions, which they both answered easily. Then they were taken into different rooms and were questioned again, mostly the same questions. She gave the same answers over and over again.

It was past one in the morning before she finally saw Beau again, and she could tell his patience was wearing just as thin as hers was.

"Are they going to let us go?" she asked.

He nodded and wrapped his arms around her. "Yes, finally. Leo and Gordy came in as well as a few others from the resort and confirmed that I was there with you. They even have video." He rolled his eyes. "Whoever was trying to set me up did a shit job of it," he added. "Let's go. Kailani's waiting for us outside."

They walked down the hallway and when they stepped into the lobby area, Kailani and a few others were waiting for them. Kailani wrapped her arms around Beau the moment he stepped into the lobby. Then she stood back as he hugged every single person who had come out to defend him.

"Let's go," Kailani said when it settled down. "They wouldn't let me get anything off the boat, so I'm afraid all your stuff is stuck onboard until the boat is out of impound."

"They impounded her?" Beau asked with a groan.

"Yeah." Kailani sighed. "Matt has had the gift shop send up some things for you, and I've set aside the penthouse across from ours for you. Don't get too excited." She held up her hands. "It's only for tonight, since it's booked out for the next week."

"Thank you," Beau said, wrapping his arms around her.

"I'll let you get some sleep, but we'll have to talk in the morning," Kailani said as they walked out.

"Right." He took Nicky's hand in his. "It looks like I won't be taking your team out tomorrow."

"No," she sighed. "I don't think I could go out even if I wanted to. I'm far too tired."

They rode in silence back to the resort and were shown up to the top floor of the four-story building. The room was absolutely gorgeous, but she didn't really care. She donned the resort T-shirt and cotton shorts that had been delivered and fell into bed next to Beau.

He pulled her close, and she shifted until she could rest her head against his shoulder.

"I'm sorry this happened," Beau said softly.

"This wasn't you," she said with a yawn. "It wasn't you," she repeated, and then she fell into a deep slumber.

CHAPTER THIRTEEN

The sound of the first explosion was deafening. His ears rang, his head spun, and every fiber of his body tensed. When the second explosion hit, he was ready for the dust, the dirt, and the sound. Still, it shocked him to know just how close it was.

His hands, elbows, and knees all ached from the cuts as he clawed his way through the rubble.

Chancing it, he glanced up and was shocked to see Tomas Rubio's body blocking his escape. The man's pale face was mocking him. His dark unseeing eyes laughed back at him as the red blood continued to ooze from the large slit in the man's throat.

It was that blood that had Beau realizing this wasn't really happening. There hadn't been blood oozing from the man's neck. The blood that had been splattered around his boat had been fresh and for show. It was obvious it hadn't come from Tomas.

With a start, he jerked awake, dislodging Nicky from his chest.

"Are you okay?" she asked in a groggy voice.

"Yeah." He walked over to the large windows, opened the glass door, and stepped out into the fresh morning air.

He wasn't used to sleeping in the chilly air-conditioning. The moment the fresh air hit him, he felt more stable.

When Nicky's arms wrapped around him, he sighed and turned to wrap his arms around her.

"I didn't mean to wake you," he said into her hair, enjoying the smell of it as much as the salty warm Hawaiian air.

"Bad dreams?" she asked.

"Memories." He sighed. "Mixed with... last night." Normally, he wouldn't have told anyone except the counselor he chatted with once a month. But this was Nicky, the first person he'd felt he could open up to since that day.

She leaned back and glanced up at him. "Want to talk about it?"

He thought for a moment then sighed. "What I want is to go for a run on the beach." He glanced down at her. "Do you think you're up for it?"

She thought for a moment, then nodded. "My shoes were on your boat."

He smiled. "I bet we can get you a pair downstairs. I'll need some too."

"Okay." She nodded. "I could go for a run."

She pulled her hair up into a ponytail, put on the swimsuit she'd worn under her clothes the day before and then pulled back on the shorts and T-shirt she'd worn to bed. She followed him downstairs.

In the store in the lobby area, they both found a pair of tennis shoes before heading out to the beach.

They walked to the edge of the water, stretched, and then took off at a light jog. He normally would have sprinted every few minutes, but with Nicky by his side, he kept a steady pace.

They ran to the curve of the beach where the jagged black rocks jutted out, blocking their path, then turned around and headed back to the resort.

About a quarter of a mile from the resort, he slowed down, and they cooled off and walked the rest of the way back.

"Feel better?" she asked him, taking his hand in hers.

"A lot. How about you?"

She laughed. "I've just realized that I need to go jogging more often."

He smiled. "I try to go at least twice a week, but most often its only once a month," he admitted.

"Want to grab a yogurt before heading upstairs?" she asked as they passed by the little shop that sold pre-packaged food.

"Sure." They stepped inside just as Jake and the blonde were heading out.

"Oh," Nicky said, almost bumping into the blonde. "Sorry."

Beau watched Jake's expression, looking for the embarrassment of being caught in the act, but the man looked proud.

"There you are," Jake said, sounding annoyed. "I heard your boat got repossessed. I'm looking into—"

"It didn't get repossessed," Nicky jumped in. "We found Tomas Rubio last night."

Jake looked surprised and excited. "You did?" He took a step forward, a genuine look of surprise and eagerness passing over his face.

"Someone murdered him and left him on Beau's boat to frame him for murder," Nicky told him.

Jake frowned and then his eyes narrowed slightly as he looked over at Beau. "Why would someone want to frame you?"

Beau shrugged. "Good question." He'd had a few thoughts on this, but until something solid came to light, it was best to keep his mouth shut.

"We spent the night at the police station. Everyone else, including Leo and Gordy, showed up to confirm that Beau was in the dining room and with me the entire time when Tomas was moved to the boat and Luano was attacked," Nicky said. "Where were you?"

"In my room, asleep," Jake said, sounding offended. "Enough of this. Is this why you're not out on the water today? Glenn's crews left at sunup."

"The *Ho'omau* was impounded," Nicky answered. "We were going to talk to someone about that this morning."

"Impounded?" Jake laughed. "It was sitting there when I met Glenn's crew."

"Why aren't you out on the water with them?" Nicky asked.

Jake's eyes filled with anger and turned towards him. "Because of your boyfriend here. No one on this island, I'm told, will allow me to dive."

Beau smiled. "Word gets out when you do foolish things. No one wants to risk their lives. Not for what you pay, at any rate."

"Did you tell them the coordinates?" Nicky asked Jake.

"Of course not. I haven't told them anything. When you didn't show up, they decided to head out near the site anyway and dive." Jake shrugged. "Apparently, no one is willing to go out tomorrow because of the storm and they didn't want to waste the day."

The entire time they'd been talking, the blonde had

stood by, looking quite bored. Beau had been watching her and the only time she'd shown interest in the conversation was when Nicky mentioned the coordinates.

"We'd better get going," Beau said to break up the conversation. "I'd like my boat back." He took Nicky's hand and walked into the store.

"Something just doesn't add up," Nicky said once they had some food and were sitting out in the pool area.

"About what?" he asked.

"Jake. I mean, why would Glenn's team waste a day diving without knowing the coordinates to the cave?" She scanned the pool area, as if she was deep in thought.

He smiled. That's what he liked about her. She questioned everything. "You like puzzles, don't you?"

She turned and looked at him, then smiled. "Who doesn't?"

"We have the next few days off. Let's put Jake, Glenn, and the treasure aside." He took her hand. "Let's enjoy ourselves. If we can," he added quickly. "We'll head in after a quick dip in the pool and get authorization to head out to my place for the storm."

Nicky nodded and her expression relaxed. "I could use the time off. I haven't had a vacation in..." She tilted her head. "A while."

"With the storm coming, it may not be much of a vacation." He chuckled. "The weather may keep us locked inside."

She leaned over and lowered her voice. "That is exactly what I am hoping for."

He pulled her closer and kissed her. He wanted to take her upstairs instead of jumping in the pool.

They got a ride to the police station from the resort's

tourist bus, which left every half hour and traveled from the resort into town and back.

At the station, he found Jay and, to his surprise, was informed that they no longer had need for his boat and that he was free to take it out.

"Just to warn you, we had to remove the sofa and a few other things as evidence. But the coroner has confirmed that Tomas was killed almost two days ago," Jay said.

"And all the blood?" Nicky asked.

"Pig's blood," Jay answered. "You will get the pleasure of cleaning the rest up," he added with a shrug. "Sorry."

Beau nodded. "Do you need to know where I was two days ago?"

"No, Kailani supplied us with your work schedule. Until we have an exact time of death, it's all we need from you. Will you be heading home for the storm?" Jay asked.

Beau nodded. "Nicky was going to come along with me."

Jay's eyebrows shot up, then he smiled slowly. "Well, be safe. Aloha." He rushed to answer the phone that was ringing on his desk.

"Well, I guess that settles that," Beau said, turning to Nicky. "Shall we head out?"

She nodded and took his hand. They rode the shuttle back to the resort. Since they had checked out prior to leaving, and all of their things were already on the boat, they made their way to the docks.

It was just after lunchtime when they got there, and he was surprised to see Glenn's crew standing around on the dock, arguing with Glenn himself.

He recognized a few of the men. Two of them were local expert divers who ran their own charters off Honolulu.

Instead of stopping at the *Ho'omau*, he diverted to the

other dock and walked up to shake hands with Charlie and his son, Pali.

"Aloha," he said easily, interrupting the argument. "Problems?" He locked eyes with Glenn.

"No, no problems," Glenn replied with a sharp tone. He stepped forward.

Pali stepped around Glenn. "We're trying to work things out now," Pali, always the pacifist, said easily.

"It sounds like what the lieutenant governor needs is another crew," Charlie said, putting a hand on his son's shoulder. "Because we can't and won't work for free."

"Free?" Beau frowned and turned to Glenn.

"The deal I've made with Charlie and Son's charter is between us," Glenn countered. "And it's not free," he added, turning to Charlie.

"Nor is it enough to pay for my crew to poke our heads in every hole in the coral," Charlie said.

Beau realized what was happening. Jake hadn't given Glenn the coordinates, so he had hired Charlie and his team to blindly dive into any and all coral caves. A very stupid and dangerous plan.

"It's enough to do the job. If you won't, then I'll hire—" Glenn started.

"Fine," Charlie broke in. "I think you should find another crew." He turned to go, pulling his son with him.

Glenn jumped in. "Fine, I'll double what I'm paying you." Charlie didn't even stop. Glenn wasn't stupid. He knew that Charlie and his crew were the best salvage crew on the islands. "Triple," Glenn threw out when Charlie reached his boat.

Charlie paused and looked back at him. "And the twenty percent finder's fee?"

"That treasure belongs..." Glenn started but when

Charlie stepped on board his boat, he threw out, "Fine. Ten percent."

Charlie stopped and looked down at his son for a moment. "Eighteen?" he called back.

"Fifteen," Glenn countered.

Charlie stepped back on the dock, walked over to Glenn, and shook his hand, which was as good as any written contract.

Then Glenn turned to Nicky. "So when is your boss going to give us those coordinates?"

"How the hell should I know." Nicky shrugged. "You'll have to ask him," she added easily. She turned to him. "Ready to go?"

He nodded and took her hand.

"What was that all about?" she asked once they were standing just outside his boat.

"That was a renegotiation."

"I'm not talking about the monetary portion of the conversation. I'm talking about the caves. Jake was adamant that we not tell a soul about the possibility of the treasure being found in a cave."

He thought about it for a moment and winced. "That might be my fault." He turned to her. "In my quest to get Jake banned from putting others in danger, I mentioned that we had been in a cave when the incident had happened."

She nodded and sighed. "Okay, now that makes sense." She smiled. "See, one puzzle solved already." She wrapped her arms around him. "I know how word spreads on small islands. I'm sure that's it." She lifted to her toes and kissed him. "I'm looking forward to putting work behind us."

"Me too." He took her hand.

"First, I guess we need to clean up some dried pig

blood," she said, causing him to groan. "I'll clean the blood while you get us heading out."

"Deal." He brushed his lips across Nicky's and thought about how much he was looking forward to spending the next two days with her.

CHAPTER FOURTEEN

C leaning up dried pigs' blood was no easy task. The space where the built-in sofa and the coffee table had sat was completely caked with dried blood.

With neither of those items there, she was able to use the hose that Beau had given her to clean the open space, along with the squeegee mop he used to clean the deck outside. She realized that, all in all, the interior of the boat was probably easy to clean since there weren't any carpets and every surface was waterproof.

"Done?" Beau asked her when she joined him upstairs.

"Yes, the *Ho'omau* is now pig-blood free." She smiled. "You'll need a new sofa and coffee table, but..." She shrugged.

"I'll order them or see what's available at Moe's." He glanced over at her. "Local boat supply shop in Honolulu."

She frowned. "You..." She glanced around and realized they were in the middle of the ocean, and she could see land far off in the distance in front of them. "I thought your place was on Maui?"

He shook his head. "Nope, in Honolulu, on O'ahu," he said with a smile. "Is that a problem?"

"No." Of course, she thought, that's why he stayed on his boat when he worked for the resort. "No problem." She wondered what other things about him she didn't know. "About how much longer?"

He glanced down at the computer screen and then tapped the GPS screen. "Half an hour or so."

She noticed a red dot on the screen and assumed that was his home. Leaning in, she looked at the map. "You live on the beach?"

He chuckled. "The house is up on the hillside, but yeah, it's waterfront property. I have a place for *Ho'omau*." He tapped the steering wheel. "My plan is to have a boathouse built soon."

"You acquired the place from Mateo? Kailani's brother?" she asked, hoping he would continue the conversation.

"Yes." He nodded. "Mateo inherited the place after their father passed. They lost their mother to cancer when they were young. It was one of the things we bonded over as kids. We'd both lost a parent. Since my mother was always at work and their father was always on the base, we stuck together." He shrugged. "I lived less than a mile away and we always seemed to meet up. Kailani moved to Maui shortly after graduation and then married Matt, so the house went to Mateo. When he graduated and joined the army, it sat empty. In that time, the needed repairs piled up. When I returned, Mateo allowed me to live there and, within a few months, he decided to let me take it off his hands. I've done most of the major repairs already. Still working on getting through my list though." He stopped and motioned to a spot just off the front of the boat. "Dolphins."

She glanced up just in time to see a spinner dolphin fly through the air.

"Wow, they're so amazing." She leaned forward to watch the pod play in front of the boat.

"What about you?" he asked her. "You have an apartment in the city?"

She laughed. "Studio apartment. One room that I pay way too much for." She thought back to everything she had worked so hard for and realized that the boat was easily four times the size of her apartment. "It does have a nice view," she added with a chuckle. "If you lean the entire top part of your body out the bedroom window."

He chuckled. "The last place I had, in Nashville, where I was stationed, had a view of a strip club's back door." He shook his head. "Let's just say I was thankful when my orders came in. I could have stayed on base, but..." He shrugged. "I liked a little freedom."

"Why did you join up then?" she asked, curious. When he looked at her, she shrugged. "You just don't seem the type. I mean..."

His chuckle stopped her. "I joined up because my father was military, my uncle is military, and it was the best and fastest way out of Wyoming."

She smiled. "I get that. I love Colorado, really, I do, but after graduation, I needed the warmth. Needed the city."

It grew quiet for a moment as they drew closer to the island. He maneuvered the boat around a few tourist-driven pontoon boats and jet skis.

"This area is crazy some days." He slowed the engines down. "I'm just around the bluff." He motioned ahead.

The farther they got away from the main port, the less traffic there was. The buildings on the land became farther and farther apart. The big resort hotels turned into crowded smaller homes, which in turn changed to large estates with pools, tennis courts, and massive boats sitting along long private docks.

Then they rounded the bluff and entered a small channel on an inlet. The land continued around the bluff, but Beau turned into the channel.

The entire hillside was fields of green surrounded by dark black lava cliffs.

"There she is," Beau said with a smile. "*Wahi maluhia.* My home." He nodded. "The highway juts back and this is the only strip of land where you can't see it from the water." He smiled over at her. "Which is nice, since you don't get the tourists driving through your backyard every day. Plus, most homes only have beach access. The water isn't deep enough for a dock. I have both."

The first house she noticed was nothing more than a speck in the distance. She could see a dirt road leading between it and its nearest neighbor, a massive home closer to the water.

Beau aimed for a shorter dock that hung off a small cliff near a small private beach. There were stairs leading to the beach and a pathway cut through the brush and trees that no doubt led up to the home.

It took her a moment to realize that Beau was talking about the massive home, instead of the smaller one in the distance.

"Is that Glenn Palakiko's place?" She motioned to the home in the distance.

Beau glanced up and nodded. "He's only there a few weekends a year. Still, he's there enough to cause problems. The last time, he took out part of my dock when he tried to dock his mega yacht. It wasn't even the first time I'd had to tell him not to use my dock."

"Does he have access to the water?" she asked.

"Not legally. Which is why he was so interested in my property. He has plans to build a giant mansion on the hillside, but he won't move forward without access to the water. He wants the dock and the beach all to himself." Beau slowed the engine even more as they approached the dock.

"You own all that?" she asked.

"Yup." He turned and, to her surprise, he cut the engine and jumped up and started walking out as they continued to float directly towards the dock.

She sat there, shocked and worried that they were going to take out the dock, but he rushed to the front of the boat and guided them safely along the dock, directly into the spot made for it. She relaxed when he tied the first rope around a thick wood beam on the dock and all motion stopped.

She stepped out onto the deck and watched as he finished securing the boat. He said something about taking longer to make sure it was secure for the storm, as he tied extra ropes to the hull before turning to her.

"Welcome to my home," he said when he was done.

The house was a lot closer than she'd first thought. The pathway that led from the beach and dock to the home was wide and had lights for after dark.

Beau carried her bag and told her that he left all his things onboard.

"No one will mess with your boat there?" She glanced up and down the shoreline. There were a few other properties on either side and several more docks with boats in the distance.

"No," he said. "Besides, after the first encounter with Glenn, I had security cameras installed." He shifted her bag so he could take her hand. "This is my garden." He stopped and showed her a small, fenced area. There were a bunch of different plants and vegetables growing inside. "I plan on getting a few chickens, maybe some goats." He shrugged and they started walking again.

Stone walls rose on either side of the pathway, directing them upwards towards the house.

The first thing they came upon was a massive swimming pool that sat off the back of the home. A large, covered porch area sat directly between the pool and the home.

She remembered him telling her that he'd built it all himself.

"You built this?" she asked, amazed at its beauty. There was a rock waterfall slide and a hot tub.

"Yes. I put in all the solar panels. They've saved me so much money already. There's an outdoor shower and a bathroom through there." He motioned to a smaller building at the edge of the pool. "We can get to the house through here," he said, and she followed him through the patio area.

She realized that they weren't yet at the house. It was on a level higher than the pool.

"The whole house is carved out of the hillside," he said as they continued to climb upward. "It's a three-story home but looks like only one story."

There was a pathway between the pool and the home. A massive deck took up the entire backside of the house.

He was correct. From the water, the place appeared to only have one story. From here, however, she could see the bottom level was hidden below the pool and patio. The deck circled the second floor while the top floor appeared to be nothing more than a single room with a wall full of sliding doors and a private deck.

"This is... massive." She shook her head. "This is where Kailani and Mateo were raised?"

"Yeah." He set her bags down, pulled out a set of keys, and unlocked the back doors. "They say that the home started out as a one-bedroom place and over the generations more was built onto it. When I first moved in, you could tell. The walls were all made with different material, so were the floors. I unified the place. Inside and out." He motioned for her to step inside. She did so, and he pushed the glass doors wide and then opened another section of door, too, so one entire side of the home was open. A soft breeze flowed through, somehow making the home come alive.

They had stepped directly into a living room. The warm tile floor of the patio continued inside, giving a seamless flow between the two spaces.

Outside, wicker furniture filled the space while inside soft blue sofas faced each other.

"There are three bedrooms on this level. The main bedroom, my bedroom, is on the top floor." Beau picked up her bag.

She smiled, knowing what he was silently asking her. "I'll stay with you," she said, and he smiled and gave her a quick nod.

"I'll give you the tour." He motioned. "This living space is nice. It's small, but perfect for guests who stay in the lower bedrooms." He motioned to a small hallway. "There's even a small kitchen space. I don't really stock it unless I have planned guests."

"Right," she said as they passed by what some would call a wet bar area. She glanced quickly into each bedroom and the shared bathroom in the hallway. They were nice.

Nicer than the bungalow she'd been staying in. Each had a queen-size bed and newer furniture.

They climbed a set of stairs made of gleaming wood and stepped directly onto the main floor. Two large glass and wood front doors sat directly to their left.

"I never really use the front door," he said with a shrug.

"They're wonderful." She admired the unique design.

"Mateo's father built them. He did a lot of the wood-work around here." Beau smiled. "He was a good man."

"He sounds like it. He had some skills."

Down a short hallway, the space opened up once more to another larger living room space. Once again, Beau set her bag down at the base of the stairs that led up and walked over to open the walls of glass.

"When I'm home, I hardly ever shut these. Unless we get a storm. We'll have plenty of time to close up before it hits us," he added with a wink.

"Were these the windows you had to wait for?" she asked as he finished opening the glass doors.

"Yes, these and the ones in the bedroom upstairs. I had to special order all of them."

This living room space had two large gray sofas facing each other along with two matching chairs. A large coffee table sat directly in the middle. Off to the side was a massive modern kitchen. There were hints of warm wood every-where—the windowsills, the doors, even the ceiling was made of long planks. She really enjoyed the warm native styling he'd chosen. It made the home feel like part of the land and the culture.

Beau was right, the entire place flowed. She could just imagine the home beginning downstairs with a smaller home, centered around the kitchen, then the second floor being added on top. She was itching to see what the third floor looked like.

"There's a dining room." Beau motioned to a side room that held a very long table.

It was then that she noticed the views. Walking over to where the glass wall had been pushed away, she gasped at the sheer beauty of the ocean beyond the green hillside that sat between the house and the water.

"Yeah." Beau walked up behind her and wrapped his arms around her. "It's a killer view."

She laughed. "This is most definitely a better view than the resort. I can see why you love it here." She sighed and dreamed of waking up in Beau's arms to this view for the rest of her life. Of feeling Beau's arms wrapped around her longer than she knew she'd be on this job.

CHAPTER FIFTEEN

Having Nicky in his house felt right. After giving her the tour, he took some fish from the freezer and they headed down to the pool for a swim. After the fish thawed, he grilled it on the grill by the pool and pulled some potatoes and fresh corn from his garden and threw them on the grill as well.

Sitting by the pool, eating fish that he'd caught and vegetables that he'd grown, hearing Nicky's laughter as she sat next to him, was one of the best feelings in the world.

They spent the remainder of the day lying around the pool he'd built. He was immensely proud of the home he'd built for himself over the past few years. But the more time he spent with Nicky, the more he realized that he'd been missing a key element.

They were enjoying cold beers on the back deck about an hour before sunset when they noticed the dark clouds off in the distance. The storm was moving fast enough that he knew they would get wind and rain within the hour.

"Is that the storm?" Nicky asked, motioning with her beer.

"Yeah, I'll need to start putting everything up, bring in the pool furniture, secure the house." He ran through his mental list of things he did whenever there was a storm.

"I can help?" she suggested.

"No, that's okay." He stood up.

She jumped up and took his hand. "Let me help."

He nodded. "Okay. I'll get the furniture down by the pool. If you would, take in all the cushions up here. There's a place for them in the closet there." He motioned to the outdoor closet where he kept everything when a storm rolled in.

"Just the cushions?"

"You can put the smaller tables inside the back doors and shut the glass doors." He motioned to the opened walls.

"Sounds good." She set her beer aside and started moving the cushions while he headed down to the pool area.

Normally the Hawaiian Islands saw about four big storms a year. He'd learned just what had to be put up and what items could withstand the weather. It was one of the main reasons he'd built the pavilion around the pool area.

The rain and the wind started shortly after dark, just as he had just finished putting all of the cushions, umbrellas, and smaller furniture in the large storage room. He quickly walked around and made sure everything else was secured before heading back up to the house.

Before he turned to the main pathway, however, he noticed a light in the utility shed where his solar batteries and equipment were kept.

Thinking Nicky must have gotten lost coming down to help him, he rushed down the pathway.

When the lights flickered on the pathway, he knew it wasn't Nicky inside the shed. He'd installed a lock on the door last year after he'd caught one of Glenn's workhands trying to get in. The man had claimed he'd wandered onto his property and had gotten lost. But Beau had wondered if Glenn had sent him there to sabotage his solar equipment.

Beau's solar panels were something Glenn had complained about since the moment he'd installed them. Apparently, Glenn could see the panels on top of the pool pavilion from his place and didn't like the look of them. Actually, he complained that the entire pavilion blocked his view. Which was a joke since his place was much higher up on the hillside. His view from up there was probably far better than his own.

When he reached the utility shed, he pulled out his phone to call the police. He didn't get a chance to, as a very large figure rushed out and a fist plowed into Beau's chin, knocking him backwards.

He landed on the gravel pathway and saw stars for a moment as the dark figured rushed down the pathway, away from the house.

It took him a few minutes to shake off the blow and get to his feet. Even then, his head spun and his vision was slightly grayed. Heavy rain had started pelting him. He stepped into the shed, holding onto the walls for support.

Using his cellphone's light, he reconnected the batteries that the attacker had disconnected. It took him longer than it should have, as he had to keep stopping because he now had double vision.

When the lights flickered back on, he glanced around and tried to assess if there was any more damage. What he needed was a security camera in the shed. Why hadn't he installed cameras all over the property? Why did he feel like he had to?

He shut the door and groaned when he noticed the cut

lock lying on the ground. He'd have to head up and get another lock. This one was completely useless now.

As he made his way back up to the house, he saw Nicky standing in the doorway, watching and waiting for him. Her arms were wrapped around herself, and he could see the worried look as he got closer.

"Are you okay?" she asked, rushing out into the rain when he stumbled at the top of the stairs to his deck.

"Yeah," he said as they stepped inside out of the rain. He shut and locked the glass doors, blocking out the rain and the wind.

"You're bleeding," she gasped when he turned away from her. "There's blood on your shirt."

He nodded. "Yeah, I caught someone messing with my solar equipment and he jumped me. He took off before I had a real chance to look at him. He sucker punched me and I fell back, and my head hit on the ground pretty hard." He reached up and felt the blood and the gravel imbedded in his skin. "I'll need to get another lock and head down there and lock the shed up again," he said as he sat down.

Nicky's hands were tugging at his shirt so that she could get a better look at his shoulder for some reason.

"Did you lock the doors downstairs?" he asked, wanting to make sure they were safe. That she was safe.

"Yes, it's all locked up. I checked. You have bits of gravel stuck in your shoulder," she said after she pulled his wet shirt off.

"Yeah." He was trying to figure out where he'd put the extra locks that he'd purchased but was too tired to think clearly.

"Beau?" Nicky said, and he realized that it sounded as if she were in a tunnel.

"Shit," he groaned before passing out cold.

When he woke, he was lying facedown on the sofa. The storm was raging outside, and he could hear the wind and the rain pelting the glass. The occasional lightning lit up the room.

"Nicky?" he asked with a groan.

"Shh, I'm here," she said directly behind him. "Just cleaning your cuts. You have a pretty big knot on your head."

It was then that he felt her fingers on him. Her touch was so gentle that he relaxed back and drifted in and out of sleep while she cleaned his shoulder and the back of his head.

The next time he woke, he'd been turned slightly on the sofa, and she was lying in his arms, fast asleep. The storm continued to rage outside.

His arm was completely asleep and, even though he didn't want to wake her, he shifted and pulled her into his arms and started to carry her upstairs.

"Sorry I fell asleep," he said to her when she stirred.

"How are you feeling?" she asked, wrapping her arms around his shoulders.

"Better. Thanks, Nurse Nicky." He smiled down at her as she chuckled.

"I've cleaned up a cut or two of my brother's," she admitted with a shrug as he crawled into his bed with her, clothes and all.

"It sounds like the storm is still raging," she said with a sigh.

"Yeah, the worst of it will hit mid-day tomorrow."

"This isn't the worst of it?" She shifted in his arms to look up at him.

He ran his fingers through her hair as he shook his head. "No, you'll know when the worst of it hits. The entire house shakes." He smiled. "God, I love a good storm."

"You do?" She shifted again and this time looked down at him.

"Sure. Don't get me wrong. I love the perfect days too, but a storm reminds you how fragile life is. It makes you appreciate those perfect days even more." He ran his hand over her hips.

Her eyes moved down to his lips and then back up and he smiled.

"I never thought of it like that. Aren't you worried? I mean, someone did just attack you. Something bad could happen," she said. "While you were out, I thought of calling the police."

"They have enough on their hands with the storm. Besides, whoever attacked me did what they came here to do," he said, shifting.

"Which was what exactly?"

"Deliver the message." He sighed and leaned down to kiss her. "We're safe. I promise." He rolled slightly until she was tucked under him. Her soft body was so warm under his, her lips inviting as he brushed his own over them.

"That wasn't how I planned to end the day." He shifted to settle between her legs.

"No?" She smiled up at him. "Show me how you had planned to, then."

He smiled and slowly started to remove her shirt and the swimsuit she wore underneath.

Since she'd tugged off his shirt earlier, he tossed his shorts onto the floor with her clothes until they were completely naked, wrapped in each other's arms.

"This," he said as he slid into her, "is how I want to spend the rest of my nights."

CHAPTER SIXTEEN

Beau's words played over and over in her head as she drifted off to sleep. She wanted that too. Wanted to be with him. To spend each night making love to him, sleeping against his body, falling asleep listening to his heartbeat.

But reality was just like the storm that woke her early the next morning. Reality came crashing in and forced her to break the dream.

The sound of distant glass breaking had both of them jumping from the bed.

"Stay here," he said. He pulled on a pair of shorts and quickly disappeared.

Her heart was racing, and she was worried about what was going on, so she climbed out of bed and pulled some fresh clothes from her bag. She was just about to go find Beau when he returned.

"What was it?" she asked.

"A branch took out the downstairs bathroom window. I'll have to board it up." He pulled on a T-shirt.

"I can help," she offered, but she desperately wished for a hot shower and some food.

"No." He walked over to her and kissed her. "I've got this. I need to go put another lock on the shed too. You go back to bed or... do whatever," he said when she gave him a look.

"I was thinking of taking a shower and then cooking you some breakfast."

He kissed her again. "Sounds good. The kitchen should be pretty well stocked still. I've only been gone about a week," he said before he left again.

Had it really only been a week since she'd watched him cross the beach? No, she thought as she stepped into the shower. It couldn't be. It felt like she'd known him much longer.

Even now, she felt so comfortable being around him that she hadn't even thought twice about staying with him during the storm. Not to mention she trusted him with her life each time they dove.

She climbed out of the shower as the storm raged on outside and dressed in a tank top and fresh shorts. Since it had been a week since she'd arrived, she decided to utilize his laundry room. She carried some of her things downstairs, along with the clothes he'd been wearing the night before, and dumped them into his washing machine after treating the bloodstains on his shirt with the stain remover she found in a cupboard.

Then she made her way to the kitchen and searched through his fridge and pantry. She could hear him banging downstairs and figured he was sealing up the window.

She found some pancake mix, almond milk, and frozen ham slices and got to work making breakfast, making sure to load and turn on his coffee machine first.

When he finally made it into the kitchen, breakfast was ready, and she had a hot cup of coffee waiting for him.

He'd obviously changed into dry clothes again, but his hair was wet. She figured it was from the rain and not the shower since he'd come up from downstairs.

"How did it go?" she asked.

"Fine. The plywood will last until I can get another window ordered." He sat down and sipped his coffee. "This looks good." He motioned to the spread.

"I would have liked something fresh from your garden but didn't want to head out in that." She motioned towards the darkened windows. She knew that the sun was up, as it was past nine already, but with the rain and the clouds, it was still so dark outside.

"Let's hope it survives," he added. "Three storms ago I lost most of what I'd grown." He shrugged as he took a bite.

Sitting at the table, surrounded by darkness, she could just imagine that this was her life. Here, with him. Secluded. With the real world outside.

During breakfast, she allowed her mind to wander, to dream. And in those dreams, the vision of her own self shifted.

She loved being an investigative journalist. Really, she did. She loved traveling, meeting new people, uncovering the mysteries that some tried to hide. She had always seen herself doing that job. But secretly, she'd wanted something more. Something she'd always believed was unattainable.

Sitting across from Beau now, in the fantasy world her mind had created, she started thinking about that possibility. The hope of becoming a writer. Sure, she wrote for her job now. Most of what she said on camera she wrote herself. But it was all facts. Things that had happened to others. What she dreamed about was telling stories.

Then she thought about Beau. He'd mentioned that he helped Kailani out to stave off boredom and to help pay for the remodeling of his house, which, she now knew, was almost complete. So, what did he plan on doing? What were his dreams?

"What did you do in the military?" she asked, curious. "Skill wise."

He shifted slightly. "Special ops," he answered, and she noticed that he no longer looked uncomfortable talking to her about his past.

"Any particular skills?" she asked, trying again.

He shrugged. "Nope, just..." He shook his head. "Nope."

"What's in Beau's future?" She leaned her elbows on the table and looked at him. "You've built this beautiful place." She motioned around. "Plan on enjoying it all by yourself for the rest of your life?"

He smiled. "That's the plan." She narrowed her eyes and took a deep breath. Then he laughed and mimicked her pose by leaning on his own elbows. "Trying to investigate my future dreams?"

"Yes," she answered truthfully. "What does Beau want to be?"

"I'm what I want to be," he answered easily.

"Which is?"

"Free," he answered, his smile slipping.

She nodded her head. "I get that. You obviously have the means to live like..." She motioned around them again. "You fill your time with fixing up the place, though at this point I can't see anything that still needs to be done. With the exception of a new window." She smiled. "You also help Kailani out, so you are not lonely, since you seem to know everyone on the islands."

"Okay, what was the question again?" he asked with a smile.

She chuckled. "What does Beau want? In a year, five years, ten years, what is Beau doing?"

"This," he sighed. "I'm right where I want to be."

She frowned. For some reason that answer didn't sit well with her. Sure, he was living in paradise. But to what end? His nearest neighbor was a pain. He had to boat to work. He didn't even own a car. What if he wanted to head to town for... eggs?

"How do you grocery shop?" she asked out of the blue. He laughed and she added quickly, "You said you don't own a car."

"I have a scooter that gets me where I need to go and can carry enough groceries for an entire month. When I use the basket." He smiled his contagious smile. "What do you say we take our coffee into the living room and watch the show?" He motioned to the windows. "It's about to get good."

"You really are excited about the storm." She shook her head, then stood up and took the dishes to the sink while he refilled their mugs.

They worked on cleaning the dishes together and she had to admit, it felt good working alongside him.

By the time they moved into the living room, the wind was so loud, it was almost impossible to hear.

"What happens if one of these windows break?" she asked.

"They're impact rated."

"What does that mean?"

He smiled. "It means they won't break. It's one of the reasons I had to wait a long time for them to be delivered. They're probably the strongest thing on the house. The roof will probably come off before these suckers will break." He sipped his cup.

"That is not very reassuring," she said, glancing towards the roof. Beau laughed and pulled her close until she was leaning against his chest, watching the rain pelt the glass.

While the storm raged on outside, he filled her in on his past, growing up with a step-sister who, according to Beau, loved Wyoming with all of her heart.

"Kara is a rancher. Through and through." He was stroking her hair as he talked, his eyes glued to the darkness outside. Still, he looked so relaxed about the storm that she felt at ease about it too.

"She's younger than you?" she asked him.

"She just turned twenty last month. We'd both been raised as only children, and when our parents met and married, suddenly we had each other." He chuckled.

"I take it things didn't go well?" she asked.

"No, just the opposite. It was as if we both appreciated having a sibling in our lives. We talk at least once a week."

"Is she married? Kids?"

"No, still single and, according to her, ready to mingle." He rolled his eyes. "She's a dork. But I love her. What about your brother?" he asked her.

"I heard from my mother yesterday. Justin and Claire are traveling together. My brother has decided to finish her trip with her." She wiggled her eyebrows as she looked up at him. "So, I assume things are going well for them."

"Claire is your best friend?" he asked.

"Not really. I mean, she's a friend I had growing up. But really, she and Justin were besties." She smiled and leaned back against his shoulder. "Their friendship was never romantic. But everyone had their hopes. Especially my mother."

"I'd like to meet them," he said easily.

She chuckled. "Oh, I'd like that too, except the moment

that happened, my Italian mother would start planning the wedding." She laughed nervously and noticed that Beau only smiled. "What about your mom?"

"What about her?" he asked, setting his empty coffee mug down.

"Does she come back to the islands often?" she asked, feeling slightly nervous.

"Twice a year. "She's due for a trip next month for my birthday."

"It's your birthday soon?" she asked, setting her own mug down.

"I'll be twenty-five on the eighth," he supplied. "When is yours?"

"October tenth."

He shifted slightly and then asked her, "You mentioned an ex-boyfriend I need to beat up. Want to fill me in on what happened?"

She chuckled then sighed. "James." She thought back to when she'd been desperate to have someone in her life. "I thought I had to have someone to be happy. I fell for James' charm and"—she rolled her eyes— "the fact that he seemed to have it all together."

"Seemed?" Beau asked.

"He drove around in this expensive car. Owned several gyms. From the outside, he had it all together."

"And the inside?" Beau asked.

"Not so much. He was a controlling narcissist who had very low self-esteem." She tilted her head slightly as she remembered the first time that he'd smacked her. "He didn't like to be questioned or challenged in any way. He used his fists to get what he wanted, not his brain. If he ever had one."

Beau smiled. "Okay, so your typical meathead."

"He was ex-military, and I found out after we broke up that he'd been dishonorably discharged for striking his superior."

"They don't look kindly on you when you do that," Beau joked. "Where is he now?"

She shrugged. "Back in San Fran, I'd wager. When I broke things off, he eagerly moved on to someone he could control, I suspect. There should be a warning label on men like that." She chuckled. "Warning, outer image does not match the interior."

He laughed and they ended up talking for a long time as the storm continued outside. When lunch rolled around, he pulled some soup he'd previously made out of the freezer and heated it up. The potato soup was better than any she'd had before.

After lunch, they settled back down in the living room, only this time, they watched the news for a while. The coverage of the storm was on every local channel.

She must have nodded off for a while and woke when the sound of thunder directly over them jolted her.

"I'm here," Beau said easily. He'd muted the television and obviously hadn't fallen asleep like she had.

"I didn't mean to fall asleep." She stretched her arms over her head.

"It's okay." He smiled at her. "It appears that you needed the rest."

She thought back to the last time she'd taken a nap and laughed. "I guess I did."

Just then the lights flickered once before the room went dark. Beau groaned heavily.

"It could be just the power," she suggested.

"One of the reasons I have solar is to keep the power on during storms." He shifted and started to get up.

"No, this time we'll go together."

"No." He shook his head. "Whoever is out there won't refrain from hitting a woman."

"I can fend for myself." She walked over to grab the pepper spray from her purse. "I normally bring my taser, but... I couldn't take it on the plane." She shrugged.

He smiled. "Okay, together then. I have rain jackets in the closet."

They suited up in the rain gear before heading out. She hadn't prepared for the wind and was thankful Beau held onto her when they stepped outside.

"Steady," he said, holding onto her.

"Thanks," she said as rain pelted her face.

Beau reached up and pulled the hood of the jacket over her face a little more, blocking out most of the water. Then he took her hand, and they made their way down towards the pool. She hadn't seen the small hut he'd been talking about the day before. It sat off to the side, between the pool and the garden. They stepped inside, and he shined his flashlight around. She saw solar power equipment and the pool equipment too.

"Someone's removed all the wire connections," Beau said with a sigh. "They cut my new lock off too."

"Why? Why would they keep doing this?" she asked him.

"My guess is..." He thought about it, then frowned. "I have no clue." He shook of his head. "I'm going to check that whoever did this is long gone. You stay put." Before she could argue, he disappeared out the door.

She bit her lip and counted the seconds until he came back.

"There were footprints in the mud. I'm sure they're gone," he said easily.

"What now?" she asked, motioning to the racks of batteries all sitting there unconnected now.

"I've got spare connections." He walked over to a cabinet. "Sometimes mice chew through the wires." He unlocked the steel cabinet and pulled out the connections. "Hold this for me?" he asked, handing her the flashlight. She held it while he worked and continued to glance towards the door, slightly afraid that whoever had done this would come back.

The moment Beau finished, the lights flickered on.

"It's that easy?" she asked, surprised.

He chuckled. "It is now. When I installed all this, there was a learning curve." He shrugged. "I should have put all this closer to the house." He groaned. "I brought another lock, but it appears as if they have heavy duty bolt cutters." He bent down and picked up the last lock, which was snapped in two. "There's nothing stopping them from just bashing in the door either." He tested the wood door. "I'll install a camera and maybe some motion lights..." He was talking to himself, but she still admired his thought process.

"What about the police?" she asked.

He glanced up at her. "Sure, yeah, I'll give them a call when the storm is over." He shrugged and tossed the busted lock in a box on the shelf.

"It's a good thing they didn't do any real damage."

"Right." He was frowning again.

"It's almost as if this was a distraction," she said when they stepped back outside.

"Yeah, my thoughts exactly, but why?" He held onto her as they made their way back up the now-lit pathway.

They were almost to the steps of the deck when she felt Beau tense. "Someone's in the house." He motioned to the windows.

She saw a shadow pass by the window upstairs and felt every one of her muscle tense.

"Here." She pulled out the pepper spray and handed it to him.

"Go down and stay under the stairs out of the rain, he whispered. "I'm going in."

"No," she said, taking his hand. "Together."

She didn't want to wait outside in the storm, alone. Each time lightning flashed and thunder sounded, she jumped out of fear, and that was with him beside her. What would she do if she was forced to hide by herself, knowing he had gone inside to fight whoever it was that had broken in?

Beau thought for a moment, then nodded. "Stay behind me." He walked over to the glass doors, unlocked them, then slid them open quietly.

She knew that he'd locked up when they had left. So how had the intruder gotten in? Had they broken another window or door? These large glass doors looked untouched.

They stepped inside together. Beau shut the door behind them and locked it. "He'll have no way out," he said quietly. Neither will we, she thought but kept it to herself.

CHAPTER SEVENTEEN

Beau climbed the stairs to the top floor, hating that Nicky was determined to go with him. He wanted her somewhere safe. Instead, she crept behind him as they moved silently up the stairs.

In his mind, he already knew who was behind the break-in and the power sabotage. Glenn Palakiko had never been silent about his distaste for Beau purchasing the place from Mateo. Nor, if rumors were to be believed, did the lieutenant governor shy away from getting his hands dirty.

After the attack the night before, he knew that whoever Glenn had hired would harm anyone that got in his way. But why break into his home? What was he looking for?

The only room on the top floor of the house was his bedroom. It faced the water with a private deck that overlooked the pool area and the dock, as well as the water beyond. His bathroom was on the backside, facing the hill and Glenn's property, which sat less than a mile across the green fields. Beyond that sat a sheer cliff on the nature preserve owned by the state.

The only reason Beau could think of for why someone

would break into his house, into his bedroom, was quietly climbing the stairs behind him.

He'd lived in the house for over two years. Glenn had stooped to filing erroneous code violations or complaints against him, but he'd never sent someone to break-in. Not until Nicky.

The chance meeting with Glenn that they'd had the morning before at the docks played quickly in his head as he opened the bedroom door slowly. The man certainly knew that Nicky was coming back to his place. What could he want from her?

He pushed the door open all the way, holding the mace can ready, then stopped when he noticed Hector, his hired hand, standing in the bedroom and holding Nicky's laptop in his hands.

"Hector?" Beau dropped his guard for a split second.

He'd hired Hector right after he'd purchased the home from Mateo. The man lived just down the street, and Beau had trusted him to check in on the house and the property for over two years.

In that moment, when his guard was dropped, Hector sprinted around them, carrying the laptop.

Before he could respond, Nicky blocked the doorway, holding her hands firmly on either side as she screamed, "Drop it."

Hector held Nicky's laptop like a football. The middle-aged man had bragged often of being captain of the team back in school.

Nicky was no match for his size or skill. Still, she held her ground. He would marvel at her courage later, but for now, she had no idea how much danger she was in. Especially since it appeared Hector had no plans to slow down.

Quickly thinking, he threw his body at the larger man's,

sending them both crashing to the ground with a thud. The wind was knocked from Hector's lungs and when he recovered, he was wheezing. They briefly wrestled for the laptop before Hector abandoned it altogether and tried to escape for the door.

Using all his skills and training, he moved quickly until Hector lay facedown on floor, his arms pinned behind him.

"Stop it," he told the man when he continued to fight. "Enough. Why?" he asked him. "Damn it. Why?"

That seemed to get the man to stop struggling. He allowed Hector to gain his breath after he promised not to try running away again.

Hector and Beau sat on his bedroom floor, looking at one another.

"He just wanted the laptop," Hector said with a sigh. "He told me he'd pay me five thousand dollars. Just for the laptop."

"He who?" Beau asked as Nicky walked over and picked up her laptop from the floor.

"I don't know. It was a skinny guy." He shrugged. "I met him at the docks."

"Do you always break into clients' homes for the promise of five thousand dollars from a stranger?" Beau asked him.

Hector looked down at his hands. "No, but... I..." He glanced up at Beau. "I have gambling debts to pay off."

"So you, what? Disconnect my battery packs so you can sneak in here and steal Nicky's laptop?" Beau asked disgusted. Hector nodded. "What would you have done if Nicky had been inside?"

Hector glanced over at Nicky, who was now holding her laptop to her chest.

"I wouldn't have let myself in." He sighed. "Please, I can't go to jail."

Beau watched the man change tactics. Hector was a good guy, or at least he had been. In the two years he'd known him, he'd always been honest. This was seriously out of character.

It made sense now that he had gotten in even though the doors had been locked. Hector had his spare keys. Anytime Beau was working in Maui, Hector would swing by and check up on the place. He worked in Beau's garden, cleaned his pool, sometimes even delivered groceries. Beau had trusted the man with everything he had.

What did he do now? Call the cops? Hector had blown that trust away. For what? The promise from a stranger for money?

Beau got up from the floor and stood over Hector. "Was it you who hit me last night?" he asked.

The surprised look that crossed Hector's face answered the question before he said no. "I only disconnected the cables. I know you had spares. I just needed enough time to sneak in, grab the laptop, and go," he said, quickly.

Beau believed him and held out his hand to help Hector up. Hector looked at his offered hand. "How much do you need?" he asked the man when they stood eye to eye.

Hector's eyes moved to the ground. "I..."

"How much?" Beau asked firmly.

"Three thousand," he answered. "Laura... doesn't know."

Laura, Hector's wife, cleaned houses for a living. Beau's house was one of them. He thought about the woman, the man he'd considered a friend, and sighed in disgust. He pulled a checkbook from this nightstand and quicky wrote a check.

"You can't..." Hector started but he stopped when Beau jerked his gaze to him.

Beau held out the check. "I suspect you were to hand over the laptop in person?"

Hector nodded. "At the dock, at midnight."

"My dock?" Beau frowned.

Hector shook his head. "No, the one in town."

"I'm going with you." He handed Hector the check.

Hector looked down at the amount Beau had written the check for. A thousand over what the stranger had offered him.

"I can't take this." Hector shook his head and tried to hand the check back to him.

"But you can break into my home and steal from me?" he countered. "Take it. Be thankful I'm not calling the police and ruining your family. Be thankful I'm not firing your wife as well."

Hector's face turned pale, and he quickly tucked the check in his pocket.

"You should have come to me," Beau said, feeling his gut wrench.

"I... was desperate. They... I'm being pressured for the money. They threatened to hurt Laura." Hector put his face in his hands. "I... was desperate."

Beau thought back to all the stupid things he'd done in his lifetime. None had come close to betraying a friend like Hector had done, but since there really wasn't any property damage and Nicky's laptop was safe, he motioned to the door. "Meet me downstairs."

Hector glanced at the door then back at him. To Beau's surprise, Hector turned to Nicky.

"I would never have hurt you or Beau," he said firmly. "I'm sorry if I scared you."

Nicky nodded quickly, and Hector turned and left the room.

"I know you probably think I should call..." Before he could finish, Nicky set her laptop down on the table, wrapped her arms around him, and kissed him.

"You did a wonderful thing." She smiled up at him. "That man was scared to death that you'd call the police."

"He's worked for me for over two years." He sighed. "His wife cleans my house, for god's sake." He ran his hands through his hair. "Why on earth would he risk it for so little money."

"Most people don't have a few thousand dollars lying around," she pointed out.

"I know." He felt stupid, and lucky that he had the money. Hell, outside of his house and boat, he didn't have a lot to spend money on. He'd paid Mateo cash for the house, and with all of his improvements, the place was worth at least ten times more than it had been when he'd moved in.

The roof had been caving in on the top floor, there had been moldy carpet in the basement, and the kitchens, both of them, had been straight out of the nineteen-fifties.

Still, Hector and Laura didn't live like paupers. Their house was nicer than this place had been when he'd gotten his hands on it. Sure, it was a great deal smaller and had barely any land since there were neighbors on either side. It also didn't have direct access to the water.

"Why does someone want my laptop?" Nicky asked, breaking into his thoughts.

"Good question. What's on there?" he asked, dropping his hold on her.

"Nothing." She shrugged. "My stories, some pictures Leo forwarded to me."

Just then a loud crash of thunder shook the house, and Nicky jumped back into his arms.

"Sorry." She laughed. "Let's head downstairs." She picked up her laptop again. "I'll go through my recent files and see what I can find that would interest someone."

As Nicky went through her files, he talked to Hector and tried to come up with an idea about who the man had been that had hired him.

From the description Hector gave him, he was coming up with a blank.

They had almost six hours before midnight. His plans to have a quiet dinner and to make love slowly to Nicky vanished quickly. Now it appeared that he and Hector would be traipsing through the end of the storm into town and meeting a man about a laptop.

They decided that Hector would drive while Beau hid in the backseat. It wasn't a smart plan, but it was a plan.

He knew the town docks well. His only problem was convincing Nicky to stay behind.

CHAPTER EIGHTEEN

"Like hell I'm staying behind," Nicky said, glaring up at Beau. "I'm going with you." She crossed her arms over her chest slowly.

"No, not this time. I insist." He took her shoulders and walked her to the hallway outside of Hector's earshot. "Nicky, I don't know what kind of trouble we'll be walking into."

"Then maybe you should call the police. Have them go instead," she suggested, not wanting to tell Beau how worried she was that he was going at all.

"And tell them what? We both agreed it's a good thing I didn't call the police about Hector," he reminded her. "Besides, we don't know what the guy wanted in the first place. Did you find anything on your laptop?"

She shook her head. "There are all the photos since we've arrived, some footage that Leo had me upload to SWE's drive, but that's it." She sighed.

"Do Leo and Jake have access to them as well?" he asked her.

She nodded. "Yes, although Leo doesn't do computers. But he probably still has them on his camera drive."

"He doesn't do computers?" Beau asked her.

She shrugged. "Long story. It's one of the reasons he's retiring soon. Everything at SWE is going digital."

"Okay, so you and Jake have them. So, why you? Why your computer?"

"I'm an easy target," she suggested. "Women always are."

"I don't buy that. First off, we're all the way on O'ahu instead of Maui. Did the person travel all the way here or were they on this island to begin with?" He shook his head. "Either way, we're going to go find out. You stay put." He pulled her closer and lowered his voice. "Please?"

That please would have convinced her if the fear for Beau's life hadn't outweighed everything else.

"I'm going," she said firmly.

Beau was quiet for a moment, then looked around the house and seemed to be thinking. Then he nodded. "Okay, but you stay in the car. This is not negotiable."

She smiled. "I promise."

She dressed in the only pair of jeans she'd brought along on the trip and her tennis shoes and a T-shirt. The normally warm Hawaiian night air had cooled, thanks to the storm. She borrowed a black sweatshirt from Beau's closet to toss on as well.

He had changed too and was wearing all black. She had to admit, he looked damn sexy in it. She'd only seen him in board shorts and tank tops or T-shirts.

Now, he wore black jeans, boots, and a long-sleeved black shirt. He looked like a professional spy. Hell, during the drive into the small town, all her mind could conjure up was images of him wearing all black and saving her. Which is pretty much what he was heading out to do at that very moment.

When they climbed into Hector's beat-up sedan, Beau stopped her. "You're taking that with you?" he asked, motioning to her laptop.

"I'm not leaving it here. Unprotected. Until I know why they want this, it goes where I go."

Beau nodded and they all climbed into the car, the two of them in the back seat.

"Duck down," Beau told her when Hector slowed the car five minutes later. "I'm going to jump out here," he told her as the car stopped. "I'll circle around and be at the dock. You stay in the car. Promise?" he asked. She nodded and felt her heartbeat double. "Good, remember to stay down." He slid out of the back seat. As soon as the door shut, Hector continued driving. He went another hundred feet before parking and turning off the engine.

"Please, do as Beau says. I don't want either of you to get hurt," Hector said before getting out of the car.

She waited, and then waited. Ten minutes later, she figured she might as well have stayed back at the house. It would have been far more comfortable than lying on the floor in the backseat of someone else's car. She couldn't see or hear anything.

She crossed her arms over her chest and started telling herself that she was an investigative journalist. How many times had she put herself in danger before?

How many late-night meetings had she gone on by herself? She'd met with some very shady people. All by herself.

She waited another five minutes before sliding up into the seat. She was technically still lying down, but she could see the docks now. They were smaller than the resort's docks. There were only four or five boats. She shifted slightly and got a better look.

She could see Hector standing under the light, alone. Waiting. Where was Beau? There weren't too many places to hide. Hell, Hector's car was the only one in the parking lot.

She moved to sit up a little more when headlights flashed over her, bathing the entire car in bright lights. Ducking quickly back down to the floor, she held her breath.

Had she been seen? Did she just blow the entire meeting? Damn.

She cursed herself and her damned curiosity. How many times had it gotten her in trouble in the past? Too many. Then again, it was one of the reasons she made a great journalist.

She listened to the other car park a few feet away. A car door opened, then closed. She counted her heartbeats, waiting for any more sounds.

After two minutes, she allowed her curiosity to take over again and chanced another peek.

Hector stood under the light, with no one else in sight. Where had the driver of the other car gone? Hector was looking around as if he too was curious. Then, as she watched, the window she was looking at shattered, sending glass spraying over her. She screamed and ducked back down, unsure of what had happened. Then she heard the shots as more glass shattered around her. She covered her head and her ears as the car continued to explode around her.

Strong arms reached in the door, grabbed her, and yanked her out. She cried out, fighting the person's hold on her until Beau's voice registered in her ringing ears.

"It's me," he said over and over again. "Run," he yelled.

She was on her hands and knees just outside the car and was about to do what he asked when she remembered her laptop.

"My laptop," she cried out, pushing his hands from her.

Before she could grab it from the floor of the car, Beau took her laptop case and shoved it in her arms. "Now run," he said firmly.

They ran while shots echoed in the distance. When the sound of her breathing grew louder than anything else, Beau pulled her aside behind a large palm bush and put his finger over his mouth.

Moments passed. She didn't know how long they stood there in the dark, waiting, listening, before Beau finally relaxed.

"I think we're safe now," he said.

She relaxed against the trunk of a palm tree and sighed. Her heart had already settled down, but now her hands were shaking.

She'd thrown the strap of her laptop bag over her shoulder so she didn't have to hold it and wouldn't drop it while they ran.

Beau took her hands and held onto them. "You're cold," he said, rubbing them.

"I'm sweating," she pointed out, and he chuckled.

"Fear causes the blood to flow to where it's needed. Your hands are cold," he corrected with a smile.

"Did you see who it was?" she asked, then she gasped. "Hector?"

Beau frowned. "Last I saw him, he was running too. I'm hoping he got away like us."

"Who was that? They were shooting at us," she added.

"You didn't keep your head down," he pointed out.

"Seriously? You think that because I snuck a peek, someone shot at us? I think they came there to kill. No matter what happened. If Hector had been carrying the laptop, he would be dead back there on the dock." She jerked her now-warm hands from Beau's and started pacing.

Where were they? All she could see were bushes and trees. Thankfully, the sky had finally cleared up from the storm so there was enough moonlight to see by. There were downed palm leaves and brush everywhere. For all she knew, they could be standing in the middle of the jungle somewhere.

"You're right," Beau said finally, causing her to turn around and look at him.

Because he was in all black, if she hadn't known he was standing there, she would have missed him. Even the moonlight didn't seem to reach him now under the cover of the trees.

Then his arms wrapped around her. "I didn't get a good look at the person, but... it looked like a very skinny and short man."

Her first thought was of Jake. But then she shook it off. Jake had access to everything she did on her computer.

"Okay, let's head home," he said, taking her hand.

"From here?" She glanced around.

He chuckled. "We're only about a mile from the house."

"What if whoever shot at us goes there?" she asked.

"I doubt it. They weren't brave enough to come get that"—he tapped her laptop case— "on their own. I doubt they want us to see their face. Besides, if they had wanted to shoot us, really hit us, something tells me we wouldn't have gotten away so easily. I'll bet Hector is already heading home himself. Safe and sound."

"So, why shoot at us at all?" she asked as they started walking through the brush.

"A warning," he answered in a near growl.

"Like last night?" she asked, remembering him saying the same about whoever had hit him.

"Yes," he said as they stepped out of the brush.

To her surprise, they stood on the edge of a beach. The sound of the waves finally broke through the high-pitched sound that had dominated her mind since the realization that someone was shooting at her.

"We're about half a mile from home." He turned to her. Now, out in the open, she could see him more clearly. "Want me to take that?" he asked, tapping her laptop, which had moved around and was on her chest now.

She turned the bag until the laptop was behind her and shook her head. "No, I've got it. Thanks." She started following him down the beach.

They walked in silence and when they reached his beach, they turned up a pathway to some stairs. Just then, his phone buzzed, and he pulled it from his jacket.

"It's Hector." He looked at the message. "He's home safe. He left his car at the docks," Beau said. He typed a message.

"Do you really think it's safe now?" she asked.

He tucked his phone in his pocket and wrapped his arms around her. "Yeah. I think whoever wanted your laptop isn't done trying to get it or whatever information is on there, but for tonight... we're safe." He leaned down and kissed her. "But I'll head inside and check everything out before you go in."

She thought of walking into the house blind. At this point she was too tired to argue with him and nodded.

They stopped short of the pool area. He pulled her into

a little clearing surrounded by palm trees and bushes where a bench sat facing the house. "Stay here. I'll be back for you." He kissed her and disappeared into the darkness.

Once again, she was left waiting. Worrying.

Her eyes were glued to the house beyond. They had left enough lights on in the place that she could see into most of the rooms from where she was sitting. She would have thought she'd see Beau walking through the house, checking every room. But she didn't see him until he came walking back across the yard towards her.

"Everything's okay," he said easily.

"You're sure?" she asked, her eyes glued to the house.

"I even checked under the bed." He helped her stand up and then wrapped his arm around her as they started walking to the house.

The moment she stepped into the house, her exhaustion took over. Beau steered her upstairs, helped her remove her shoes, and set her laptop by the bed so she could remove the rest of her clothes. The moment her head hit the pillow, she was out. She didn't even see or feel Beau crawl into bed with her.

She woke to sunshine streaming through the windows and Beau looking at her from across the pillow.

"Did you sleep okay?" he asked her with a smile.

She nodded. "Yes, you?"

He nodded. "What time are you supposed to be back at the resort?"

She remembered the message from Jake yesterday and sighed. "Nine."

"It's six now. We'll just make it. We'll have breakfast on the boat."

She nodded. "I'd like a shower first."

"Of course." A slow, wicked smile crossed his lips. "The

shower here is most definitely big enough for the two of us." He raised his eyebrows, and she felt her entire body heat as she remembered how sexy he'd looked last night. How sexy he looked at the moment with his hair all messed up.

"What are we waiting for?" she said eagerly. She rolled out of bed to the sound of his laughter, and he chased her into the other room.

CHAPTER NINETEEN

Beau tried like hell to not let his dark thoughts ruin what little alone time he had left with Nicky. The fact was, he'd only gotten a few hours of sleep the night before.

He'd spent the rest of the time going over Nicky's files—every picture on her laptop, every video—until he'd found the one that he believed someone wanted.

It was one that he'd taken that day he'd had to save Jake's life in the coral cave. It was the only video of the exact cave Jake believed the treasure would be found in.

He seriously doubted that Jake or Leo had a copy, since it was in a file marked Do Not Share on Nicky's backup hard drive. Before falling asleep, he copied the video to a flash drive.

Still, the only person he could think of that might want their hands on the file was Glenn. If Jake really hadn't given him the coordinates, then the video might help locate the cave. It was a long shot, but so far, the only possibility.

While he worked on getting them out onto the water, Nicky went into the galley and made them yogurt and oatmeal.

"Sorry, we're limited on groceries," he said as he finished his meal. They were already halfway back to Maui at this point.

"It's okay. I'm sure Gordy is the reason you're out of everything," she joked.

"He does eat a lot for a skinny guy."

She laughed. "He orders two meals when we sit down for dinner meetings." Beau laughed along with her. The rest of the trip to Maui they talked about everything except for what had happened the night before. It wasn't until they could finally see the dock that she brought it up.

"What do I do now?" she asked, nodding to her laptop sitting next to her. "With this?"

"I've thought about it. There's a safe in Matt's office. He and Kailani are the only ones with access to his office and the only ones who know about the safe."

"What about my work?" she asked.

"Use my laptop. It's in my room below."

She was silent for a while and then nodded. "Okay, if you're sure it will be safe there?"

He nodded. "It will. I'll make sure that no one else knows about it."

"Thanks," she said with a sigh as they pulled into the docks.

Instead of Luano coming out to help secure the boat, Matt met them at the docks.

"I saw you coming," Matt said after securing the ropes.

Matt helped Nicky onto the dock. She was due to meet with her coworkers and Glenn's team in the lobby in less than five minutes.

"Thanks." She glanced quickly at Beau.

"I'll be here," he told her. She nodded and turned to rush inside.

"I'll help you refuel before you're due to head out," Matt said to him. While they worked on refueling and restocking, he filled Matt in on what had gone down the night before. Matt was shocked and worried, but he understood Beau's background and trusted his judgement. He explained their plan to lock the laptop in his office safe, and he agreed to keep it a secret.

Nicky had come up with the idea to hide the laptop in the bottom of a cooler for transport. This way, Matt wouldn't become a target if anyone was watching them. Matt would just be taking a cooler into his office, which wasn't out of the ordinary.

When the boat was restocked with basic supplies, he gave Matt the cooler.

Matt took the small cooler. "Can I get anything for you?" he asked.

"No, I think that's it. Nicky will be staying onboard with me again."

"It seems pretty serious between the two of you." Matt nudged him on the shoulder.

"She's unlike any woman I've ever been with," he admitted.

"What are you going to do when she goes back home to the mainland?" Matt asked.

Beau hadn't thought that far ahead. If he did, he'd start thinking about life on the mainland again and how it just wasn't possible. He couldn't imagine returning to the craziness, the speed of things, the... pressure and suffocation he felt when he visited.

"One day at a time," he answered with a shrug.

Matt nodded. "She doesn't strike me as someone who will slow down."

"No," he responded and then jumped back on board.

"Thanks for taking care of that." He nodded to the cooler. "If you have any problems, let me know."

"Will do." Matt turned and left.

He had another half hour before Nicky and her team were due to leave the dock, so he walked up to the little store in the lobby and gathered some basic groceries he was short on. They didn't carry eggs and such for customers, but he found what he needed in the kitchens. He had just finished putting everything away when Nicky and her team arrived.

What surprised him was that Jake was with them. The man acted as if he was actually going to go out on the water. As if nothing had happened before.

The look on Nicky's face told him that the man believed it was the case.

Jake tossed a huge black bag on deck and moved to step onboard. Beau blocked him.

"Where do you think you're going?" he asked the man.

"It's my crew. I can't waste another day that I'm paying for." Jake tried to move around him. Beau blocked him again.

"You're paying for your team to go out. It's not wasted," Beau pointed out. "I've made myself very clear that you're not welcome any longer."

Jake rolled his eyes. "You've made your point," he threw back at him. "I don't trust anyone else with the coordinates."

"Nicky knows them. So do I now."

Jake's eyes narrowed. "There's new information."

Beau glanced over at Nicky, who shrugged and continued to help Leo with his equipment.

"What new information?" Beau asked Jake.

"Information I'm not willing to give until we're out on the water." He motioned to Glenn's crew, who had finished loading the boat across the dock from his own. Glenn was nowhere in sight, but that was to be expected. After all, the man didn't like to get his hands dirty himself. He had doubted that he'd be going out on the boat each day, diving himself.

Jake leaned closer to Beau and lowered his voice, "I'll double what they're giving you."

Beau laughed and shook his head. "Maybe you can catch a ride with Glenn's crew?"

Jake glanced over and then back at Beau and lowered his voice even more. "I don't trust them."

"I don't trust you," he countered.

Jake was quiet for a moment. "Double pay"—he held up his hand, stopping Beau from responding— "with a guarantee that I stay out of the water."

Beau glanced over at Nicky and the rest of the crew, who all shrugged and or nodded.

Beau stepped aside, but as Jake passed by, he held out his hand. "I'll expect you to keep your word."

Jake easily shook his hand. "I will."

They set off with Glenn's crew, with Charlie at the helm directly behind them.

"Won't they have the coordinates after today?" Gordy was asking Jake.

"We're not heading to the site just yet," Jake responded.

"We aren't?" Beau asked.

"No. Not exactly. Nearby, but... just slightly off. I'd like to keep some of my cards to myself. At least for a while." Jake moved over to sit next to Beau. "Here." He handed him a small piece of paper with new coordinates on them.

The new location wasn't far from the other one. But in a big ocean, it might as well have been a needle in a haystack.

He punched in the new site as everyone got settled for

the trip. Since the sofa Leo had grown comfortable traveling on was no longer there, the man had climbed the steps and was now sitting on one of the two sofas directly behind him.

The conversation turned to Tomas Rubio's murder. The storm had blown through without any major damage, so it was apparently all anyone on Maui could talk about.

There were rumors going around and, thanks to Gordy, they heard them all during the trip.

When he finally cut the engines and dropped anchor, he was thankful to end all the speculation, especially from Jake, most of which involved him personally. Hadn't the man just said that he trusted him over Charlie's team?

It was obvious that Jake would say or do anything to get what he wanted. Just as long as the man didn't get in the water, Beau didn't really mind.

Everyone suited up and since Nicky, Gordy, and Leo would be diving with Charlie and his team, he decided to stick with the boat and Jake for this first trip.

He didn't like seeing Nicky head into the water without him, especially after what had happened the night before, but his trust in Charlie and crew was greater than Jake's was.

He'd worked with Charlie a few times over the past two years. The man was honorable enough. He loved his son, Pali, who had graduated the prior year and had started working full-time with his father shortly after. Charlie's wife had died years ago, leaving him a single dad.

"Well," Jake said, getting his attention, "now we wait."

"Why the new location?" he asked.

Jake looked slightly surprised. "I got a new tip," he finally said with a shrug.

"From?" Beau assessed the man and instantly knew he was uncomfortable about something.

"A new resource," Jake answered.

"Are you purposely being vague?" he asked. When Jake didn't answer, he added. "You did just tell me you trusted me. Remember?"

Jake sighed. "Tomas left me a message."

"When?" he asked, eager to know.

"The night we arrived. I didn't get it..." Jake shook his head. "It's new information. That's all you need to know."

"Did you tell the police?" Beau asked.

"Why would I?" Jake asked with a frown.

"They're still trying to determine when Tomas was murdered. If he left you a message, that might be the last thing he did before being killed."

Jake's face paled. "You... you think he was murdered because..." The man sat down on the bench, hard.

Jake seemed visibly disturbed about the possibility that a man had been murdered for the information he'd passed on. But maybe Beau was reading it wrong. Maybe Jake was upset because now he realized that he himself could be in danger.

Either way, it took the man a few moments to compose himself.

"How well do you trust Glenn and the crew he hired?" Jake asked him once he had recovered.

"Glenn? Not an ounce. Charlie and Pali can be trusted. I don't know any of the others on his team very well."

It grew quiet again.

"So, you and Nicky?" Jake said.

"No." He shook his head. "What's between us is not up for discussion."

Jake held up his hands. "Hey, I get that. The need for privacy." He looked off to the distance. "Jennifer, my wife, and I decided early on that we were going to be open. Not a lot of people can understand that." The man rolled his eyes.

"You do you," Beau said with a shrug. For the first time since meeting the guy, Jake smiled at him.

"Yeah, right." He leaned back. "What about Glenn?"

Beau chuckled. "Like I said, you do you."

"No." Jake frowned. "I mean, how much do you trust him?"

"Like I said, I don't. And not just because he's a politician," Beau answered.

"What's the reason then?"

"He is my neighbor. From the moment I moved in, he's caused me problems. I believe he convinced one of his workers, Joseph, to break-in to my place and do a little damage once. He denied it, but then paid the guy's bail and fees."

Jake shook his head. "Yeah, I wouldn't be working with him if I didn't have to, but unfortunately, my orders came from higher up." He sighed.

They talked for a little while longer while Beau half-listened to the diving team's chatter on the radio.

By the time they heard another boat motor heading their way, Beau had let his guard down and was actually beginning to think he'd misunderstood the man. They had both turned to watch the speedboat, which was quickly heading directly between his and Charlie's boats. It was a little too far to see who was driving, but it was clear that there were two people on board.

One was driving and one was aiming a gun directly at them.

Beau reacted quickly, ducking down below the cargo hold that held the tanks. Jake wasn't as lucky. He doubled over and fell, grasping his chest.

The back sliding glass door feet away from them exploded, sending shards of glass raining everywhere. Beau army-crawled towards Jake as the man gargled and gasped for air.

Beau counted more than a dozen shots before the explosion rocked his boat. Knowing instantly that they had hit the tanks on Charlie's boat, he briefly thought about his own, worried not only about the full fuel tank but the dozen or so oxygen tanks in the hold not far from his head.

Dragging Jake, he slipped them both off the back of the boat into the water and prayed that Nicky was safe.

CHAPTER TWENTY

Nicky did her best to keep up with the rest while carrying Leo's other camera and was thankful when they reached a spot where they could start filming.

She didn't know what Charlie and his team knew, if Jake had told them anything. Since their walkie talkies were connected, they talked the entire time as they dove.

"We're going to need to know what we're looking for," someone on his crew said.

"Treasure," she responded easily, earning a few chuckles.

"Come on, princess. Give us something," the same voice came, and she desperately wished to know who had said it.

She replied, "For now, we'll stick to the coral reef. I'll let you know when that plan changes."

Thankfully, she got no argument from any of them. They spent almost twenty minutes swimming along the coral reef before someone spotted a cave.

"What do you say, princess?" This time she saw that it was a man named Fritz. At least that's how Charlie had introduced him. She didn't know if it was a nickname or the man's real name. He motioned to the cave. "Shall we head into the cave?"

She was just about to say yes when a loud sound caused everyone to look up. They were less than a mile from the boat at a depth around two hundred feet, and everyone understood instantly that one of the boats had exploded.

The entire team turned and raced to the surface. She raced far ahead of everyone else. She remembered the warnings of what could happen to divers when they surface too quickly and knew she should slow down. The bends was no joke. But her fear for Beau outweighed caution.

She tried desperately to contact Beau over the radio, each time waiting several heartbeats for his response. She heard nothing but static over the line.

What had happened? Was it the *Ho'omau* that had exploded? Was Beau okay? The worry caused her breathing to double. She knew she was running through the oxygen quickly but didn't care. She needed to get to Beau. Needed to know that he was okay.

When they got closer to the surface, they noticed another boat speeding away from the wreckage.

She spotted the blood in the water first and told the others. They all turned to the two figures swimming at the surface near the *Ho'omau*, which, thankfully, was still intact.

Thoughts of Beau bleeding, of him dying and being seriously injured, scared her so much that she dropped the camera and swam as fast as she could towards him.

"I'm okay," Beau told her when she surfaced.

Beau was holding Jake, who was very pale. He was making a gurgling sound from deep in his chest.

"He's been shot," Beau added as they swam back towards the *Ho'omau*.

It took some doing, pulling Jake back up onto the boat.

"What the hell happened?" Charlie asked, his face pale as he looked over at the spot where his boat had been.

"Go call in an SOS to our position," Beau barked to one of the men as he put a towel on Jake's chest and applied pressure.

She removed her tanks and equipment as quickly as she could and knelt beside Jake to help out. With shaky fingers, she felt for a pulse and didn't find one. She told Beau, who immediately started CPR.

She'd never felt so helpless in her life. She knew CPR, had even kept up with her certificate. But she was clueless when it came to helping someone with a bullet hole in his chest.

Moments later, the boat started moving at a fast speed towards shore while Beau worked on Jake. Each time he pushed air into Jake's lungs, she swore she heard it woosh back out his chest as more blood oozed out.

They met the coast guard halfway back to the island. Jake was transported to their ship while one of the crew took over working on Jake for Beau.

Beau immediately collapsed back against the bench. He looked tired. More tired than she had ever seen him. Without thinking, she scooted over to him and wrapped her arms around him.

"He'll be okay," she said as tears flooded her vision.

"We had no chance," he said softly. "It was an ambush." He closed his eyes and took several deep breaths.

"You did your best to save him." She rested her head against his shoulder.

"My boat?" Charlie said once the coast guards' boat had disappeared. They had been told to wait there for another one that would guide them back to shore, where the police would be waiting to take their statements.

"They must have shot the tanks," Beau said. "I was lucky they didn't get mine." He motioned to the bullet holes that riddled his boat and storage areas. "It was as if they knew just where to aim."

"Why?" Pali asked as he sat next to his father. "Why would someone do that?"

Beau glanced down at her, and she felt her stomach roll.

"Apparently someone doesn't want us looking for the treasure," Charlie answered with a heavy sigh. "It doesn't matter now. We're off the job." He wrapped his arms around his son. "It's a good thing you convinced me to let you go with us."

Nicky's heart jumped in her chest. What if Pali had stayed on the boat? She doubted that the skinny twenty-year old kid would have been able to survive the explosion.

They waited in silence until the next coast guard boat pulled up beside them. Someone from that boat came aboard and steered the boat into the dock. Instead of heading to the resort's dock, they had pulled into a spot at the town's docks.

There were three police cars waiting for them. Beau headed to his cabin and showered off all the blood and changed into dry clothes. She pulled on a shirt and her shorts and washed Jake's blood from her hands.

They were all put into separate cars and driven to the station where they answered questions for the next two hours.

By the time she and Beau walked out of the station, she was exhausted.

Kailani was once again waiting for them, and she wrapped her arms around both of them.

"Are the two of you okay?" she asked, concern flooding her features.

"Yes," Beau sighed. "Just tired. Have you heard anything about Jake?"

"He's been airlifted to the hospital in Honolulu. From what they know, he had a steady heartbeat when they reached the shore," Kailani answered.

A huge sigh of relief escaped her lips, and Beau wrapped his arm around her waist.

"We'd like to go home. Get some rest now," he said.

Kailani nodded. "This time they let me grab your bags," she said to Nicky as they walked out of the station. "I packed a few things for you too," she told Beau.

"Thanks," Nicky told her as she climbed into the back seat of the resort's van. As Kailani drove, Nicky rested her head on Beau's shoulder.

She must have fallen asleep at one point. When the van came to a stop, she jolted awake. Instead of being in the resort's parking lot, they were stopped in front of a massive home. Two large wood beams arched over the entryway, and there were glass doors much like the ones at Beau's place.

"Kailani and Matt's place," Beau supplied. "We'll stay here until the *Ho'omau* is ready."

"Right." She followed him out of the van.

The home was in the same style as Beau's place. The house sat sideways on the lot. From the circular driveway, you could see that the home sat directly on the water, only there were no black cliffs between it and the water. Instead, a pristine green yard with a swimming pool as big as Beau's separated it from the private sandy beach.

"The resort is just down there," Kailani said as she took Nicky's bag and threw it over her shoulder. "I wanted to live close to work." She smiled. "Please, while you're here, you are *'ohana*." She opened the doors. "Beau knows where the guest room is. I'm going to head back to work." She stopped and then hugged Beau again. "Stop putting yourself in danger's way. I don't think my heart can take it," she added and then left.

"Come on," Beau said, taking her bag with his own.

She followed him down a long marble tile hallway and past a huge sunken living room with panoramic views of the ocean to the last door on the left. The guest room was beautiful, and she would have stopped to appreciate it more had Beau not dropped their bags and fallen face-first into bed.

"Come here." He patted the spot next to him. "Let's shut down for a while."

She toed off her sandals and crawled in beside him.

He rolled over and hit a switch on the nightstand, and the curtains began closing, shutting the light out of the room. Then he rolled over, gathered her in his arms, and quickly fell asleep. It didn't take her long to follow him.

Her phone woke her several hours later. Rolling over, she fumbled in her bag and answered her mother's call.

She was a little too groggy to really talk and ended up getting off the phone without telling her mother anything that had happened to her in the last few days.

"Is everything okay?" Beau asked her.

"Sorry, I didn't mean to wake you." She tossed her phone down on her bag again.

"It's okay. My stomach would have woken me soon anyway." He sat up and rubbed his hands over his face then turned to her. "You didn't want to tell your mother anything?"

She shrugged. "I'll call her when I'm a little more

awake." She yawned. "I could use a shower." She picked up her bag.

"The bathroom is through there." Beau nodded to a short hallway. "I'm going to make a few calls."

Nicky stepped into the bathroom, closed her eyes, and rested against the closed door. What was she doing? There was no doubt that she was in denial about what had just happened.

They hadn't even gotten to go into the cave earlier before someone had tried to kill them. Why? Had someone already found the treasure? Was someone trying to stop them from finding it? Nothing was making sense.

This was her job, finding answers to questions like this. So then why was she hitting a brick wall?

She tossed her bag down, walked over to the glass shower, and turned it on. When she stepped under the warm spray, her mind cleared a little.

What she wanted to do now was talk to the blonde woman Jake had been seeing. She didn't know why, but something in her gut told her there was a deeper reason that the woman was with Jake. Not that Jake wasn't an okay-looking man. But he was kind of skinny. Scrawny, some would say. He didn't have a lot of money, not that she knew of, at any rate. So why was a woman half his age who could easily be on the cover of any fashion magazine be interested in him?

Making up her mind, she made a quick call.

When she stepped out of the bathroom, freshly dressed in a summer dress with her hair in a long braid, she found Beau swimming laps in the pool outside.

Sitting on one of the wooden chairs, she waited until he surfaced.

When Beau finally spotted her, his eyebrows drew up in question. "Going somewhere?"

She smiled. "I've got an interview."

"What kind of interview?" he asked, sliding out of the water.

She quite literally lost her breath. Her mouth watered as he used a towel to dry off his toned, tanned skin.

Hearing his chuckle, she snapped out of the fantasy of running her hands, her mouth, over every inch of him.

"Sorry." She shook her head. "What?" She blinked a few times.

"What kind of interview? With whom?" he repeated.

"Jake's mistress," she answered quickly. "Something tells me the woman knows something."

Beau was quiet for a while, then nodded. "Okay, I'll get dressed." He started to head to the house.

"You don't have—" she started, but the look he gave her had her shutting her mouth. "I'll be right here, cooling off." She waved her hand in front of her face. Seeing him smile, hearing his chuckle as he walked into the house, made her smile. She leaned back to enjoy the sunshine.

Less than ten minutes later, Beau returned wearing khaki shorts and a button-up shirt.

"We can walk from here," he said, shutting the back door.

"Sounds good to me." She tossed her bag over her shoulder and followed him across the grass to the beach.

"What are you going to ask her?" he asked once they were on their way.

"Nothing pointed." She glanced sideways at him. "Thankfully, the front desk confirmed that she's still checked in and that she booked the room for another week just yesterday," she answered. "I'm not sure that she knows about Jake yet." She glanced at Beau.

"How do you think she'll respond?" he asked.

"That's what I want to see. I'm hoping word hasn't gotten to her yet. I'd like to see her honest reaction."

"Do you expect to just bump into her?" he asked.

"I talked to your Alana, and she told me that Katrina—that's her name—usually spends the afternoon at the pool. So yeah, I'm hoping to just... bump into her."

"Want me to stick around if you do?"

"I'm playing it by ear." She shrugged. "Your opinion on how she reacts would be helpful."

He nodded and then took her hand as they headed up the beach towards the pool area.

CHAPTER TWENTY-ONE

Sure enough, the blonde was lying in one of the cabanas, sipping a mai tai while reading a book.

"Here we go," Nicky said. She slipped her phone out of the pocket of her purse and hit record, then tucked it into the side pocket. Beau nodded and followed her, eager to watch her work.

"Katrina?" Nicky stopped directly in front of the woman, blocking out the sun.

The woman lifted her hand and peered at Nicky from over the rim of her dark sunglasses.

"Yes?" she responded.

Beau picked up instantly on the thick Ukrainian accent. The woman was, without a doubt, one of the most beautiful women at the resort, if you went for the plastic type. From her tiny waist to her very ample double D's, which were obviously enhanced, there wasn't a hair out of place. There was no doubt that her lips were, filled and she'd had enough Botox to stop her face from moving. Still, he doubted that any of it had been necessary.

"I think you and my boss, Jake, were here together?"

Nicky casually sat down on the edge of the chair next to the woman.

"I don't think so," Katrina said, pulling her glasses back up.

"Sure you were." Nicky waved her hand as if dismissing the woman's denial. "Well, we just stopped off to let you know that he's doing well. They've moved him to the ICU. They managed to remove all of the bullet fragments."

He knew that Nicky was bluffing. She'd told him that she didn't know Jake's current condition. While he'd been inside changing, she'd called the hospital to get an update and was told that he was still in surgery. But they agreed that this would be a better angle than just saying he was still in surgery.

"What?" Katrina frowned. Well, if you could call it a frown. "Oh no, what has happened?" She sat up. He could tell that Nicky understood that the woman was acting. Nicky's eyes narrowed slightly. Just enough that Katrina noticed and poured on the concern even thicker. "Is he okay?"

He watched the show, knowing full well that Nicky would get what she needed from the woman, no matter how skilled of an actress she was.

"Like I said," Nicky paused. "He's in recovery. Because he was shot."

Katrina made a small move. It was ever so slight, but he and Nicky noticed it instantly. The corner of her lip turned up, just a twitch. The woman was obviously happy that Jake had been shot. Actually, she looked annoyed when Nicky mentioned that he was in recovery.

"But then, you already knew that. Didn't you?" Nicky said smoothly.

Katrina surprised both by smiling and leaning back.

"Go away now." She waved her hand. "You have delivered your message."

"Aren't you worried?" Nicky asked.

"For what?" Katrina tilted her sunglasses and glanced over at him. "Him?" She laughed. "You are nothing more than an employee here, and you"—she motioned to Nicky, then laughed— "a second-rate journalist who, according to Jake, will never get that promotion you so desperately want." She pulled her glasses back up. "Go now."

"Did you shoot him?" Nicky asked her without missing a beat.

Katrina didn't say anything at first, then she sighed and poured on the drama again. "No, I would never shoot anyone. Especially my Jake. I loved him. He was going to leave his wife for me." She reached up and brushed away a fake tear. "I know nothing of what you speak. Leave me now." She waved her hands again.

"Why? Was it for the treasure?" Nicky asked, unmoved and, he would bet, unwilling to leave.

"If you will not leave..." Katrina started to get up, but Nicky blocked her path with her legs.

"Who are you working with? Did you kill Tomas Rubio?" she continued before Katrina could say anything. "Did you break into Beau's house in Honolulu? Did you shoot at us the other night at the pier?"

Katrina groaned loudly and then shoved Nicky's legs aside so that she could stand up. "I don't know what you're talking about." She gathered her things and marched away.

"That was..." Beau said, taking the seat that Katrina had vacated. "Enlightening?"

Nicky shifted until she was sitting in the chair next to him with her legs up. They both watched Katrina storm across the pool area and disappear inside.

"So, the question now is, who is she working for or with?" Nicky reached in and turned off her recording.

"You know you can't use that as evidence, right?" He motioned to her phone.

"Yeah, it's more for my benefit. In case I missed something." She shrugged.

"Like?" he asked, doubting she'd missed any of the exchange. She was always watching, listening, to everything.

"Her accent. Russian or Ukrainian?" Nicky tilted her head in thought.

"Ukrainian," he answered easily. He shrugged when she glanced at him. "I've... spent some time in both places," he answered, not wanting to get into the details at the moment.

"Right." She sighed and relaxed back. "Okay, so..." She closed her eyes. Just then he heard her stomach let out a loud growl, causing his own to complain about them missing lunch.

"Let's order some food," he suggested, waving Ann over.

"Hi, Ann. Nicky and I would like to order some sandwiches. Mahi, blackened, with fries." He turned to Nicky and asked. "Drinks?"

She nodded towards Katrina's discarded drink. "One of those."

"I'll take one too," he said. Ann nodded at them and then disappeared quickly.

"Who do you think she's working with?" Nicky picked up once they were alone again.

"Glenn," he answered easily. He'd been thinking about it for a while now. "It just... makes sense."

Nicky glanced over at him. "The lieutenant governor? I know you and him have... history, but do you really think that he'd stoop to murder? Why? When he already had a deal with Charlie and his crew?"

"Yeah, that part I can't quite figure out." He turned slightly to her and smiled. "You're the investigative journalist. What do you think?"

She was quiet for a moment, then Ann delivered their drinks and disappeared again. They each took a sip and watched a family happily splash around in the pool.

"I have a theory," Nicky finally said.

"Okay, shoot." He leaned forward and sat up

"What if... Glenn has already found the treasure?" she asked.

He frowned. "Then... why hire Charlie and his crew in the first place?"

"Hear me out. What if Tomas and Glenn knew one another? Tomas tells his good friend about the treasure. Maybe even takes him on a fishing trip." She pulled out her cell phone and swiped through the photos and then showed him the one of Tomas holding the fish up with Beau standing behind him. "There." She pointed to the arm of the man just off screen. "Look at your face." She motioned. "Whoever is standing there, you're obviously not impressed with."

He thought back, tried to remember the trip, but he was coming up blank.

"Have you ever taken Glenn out on a charter before?" she asked him.

"Sure, several times. He likes to wine and dine a few high rollers at least once a month." He sighed. "Okay, so let's assume that this is Glenn. I really can't remember," he said honestly. "And that Tomas and Glenn really did know one another. Why kill him?"

"Because he told someone else about the find," Nicky said, tucking her phone away.

Beau thought about it. "Okay, I'll buy that. If..." He held up his finger. "Glenn wanted to keep the find secret."

"You said it yourself. The King's Treasure. What happened to most of it?" she asked.

"The state of Hawaii owns it all."

"What if Glenn wants to keep a little for himself? Who would know?"

Then they both grew quiet while their food was delivered.

Before Ann left, she turned around. "I almost forgot. Someone left you this message at the front desk." She handed Nicky a note.

"Thank you." Nicky waited until they were alone again before opening it.

Instantly, she frowned down at the note.

"It's from Leo. We've been pulled off the story." She started to stand up, but he stopped her. "I need to go sort this out."

"Eat first," he said with a sigh. "I can't think straight."

She took a deep breath and nodded. They ate in silence and the moment he could think, his gut started to twist at the thought of losing her so soon.

"I'm not leaving now," Nicky said after a few bites of her sandwich. "Not when there's finally a scoop." She avoided his eyes.

"I don't want you to go," he admitted. She glanced up at him and he reached over to take her hand. "Whatever this is"—he motioned between them with their locked hands—"I don't think I want to lose it."

She smiled and he felt his heart jump in his chest as his smile doubled. "I feel the same."

"Good." He dropped her hand. "Let's finish eating so we can settle things."

When they were done eating, they went inside and found Leo and Gordy at the bar, having dinner together. Both men looked rested and eager to go home.

"There you are," Leo said when they sat next to him. "We've got flights out in the morning."

"I'm not going," she told them. "Not yet." Both Gordy and Leo glanced his way. "Think whatever you want, but there's a scoop here and I want to follow it. There's a reason someone killed Tomas and shot at us today, and I'm going to find out why."

They were silent for a while, then Leo nodded. "Normally, I'd be right there by your side, but I've put in my request for retirement. After... today." He shook his head.

Nicky reached over and touched the man's arm. "I get it." She smiled. "Gordy, you should go home too."

"You don't have to tell me twice," Gordy said with a shake of his head. "Have we heard how Jake's doing?"

"Last I heard he was in surgery," she said.

"Damn." Gordy shook his head. "Don't get me wrong. I didn't like the guy, but..." He sighed. "He didn't deserve that."

"No," Nicky agreed quickly.

"You were amazing," Gordy said to Beau. "Taking charge and saving him. Jumping in the water so you didn't blow up."

"Thanks," Beau said quickly.

"When I get back home, I'm going to take a CPR course. SWE has agreed to pay for it," Gordy added. "I have never felt so helpless in my life."

"It's a good thing to know," Beau responded. "You never know when you might need it."

"Well..." Leo finished his drink. "I'm going to head up and get some rest and pack." He stood up. "I guess I'll see you when I see you."

Nicky jumped up and hugged the older man. "Good luck. Enjoy your retirement."

"Thanks," Leo said and disappeared.

"Yeah, me too. Guess I'll take one more walk on the beach. Who knows when I'll get back here." He stood up and disappeared towards the beach.

"What do we do now?" Nicky asked Beau.

"We head back and get some rest. Then, tomorrow, we see about getting my boat back."

Taking her hand, they walked out past the pool and onto the beach.

While they'd been inside, the sun had started to sink, and he could tell it was going to be a perfect Hawaiian sunset, so they took their time getting back to Kailani's place.

When they reached Kailani and Matt's yard, he pulled her into his arms and kissed her. She laughed and hugged him then pulled out her phone and snapped a few pictures of the sunset and them together.

Whatever happened now, he didn't want those pictures to be the only thing he had to remind him of the woman he had fallen in love with.

He was desperate to come up with some way to convince her to stay with him. Beau knew that there was no way he would ever recover if she left for good. He'd lost his heart completely.

CHAPTER TWENTY-TWO

Nicky never wanted the night to end. Standing in the sand, watching the most perfect sunset she'd ever seen in the arms of the most perfect man, she knew that nothing would ever compare to that moment.

Whatever she'd thought of Hawaii when she'd first come here, those preconceptions were long gone. She had found her *'ohana*. Beau was her heart.

Wrapping her arms around his shoulders, she kissed him, pouring every feeling she had for him into the kiss.

When he leaned back and looked down at her, she lifted her hands to his face.

"Don't freak out or anything," she said with a smile, "but I think I'm in love with you."

He chuckled. "I was about to say the very same thing."

"You were?" she asked as her heart skipped a few times.

Beau nodded and then kissed her again. "Yes," he said with a sigh. "What are the chances of me convincing you to move in with me?"

"I'd say pretty good." She laughed when he looked

surprised. "First, we have to finish this story. Then we can hash out the details."

He nodded. "Agreed." He took her hand. "We'll finish the story in the morning. Tonight, I want to make love to the woman I love."

She smiled and followed him inside.

Kailani was in the living room watching the news when they stepped inside.

"There you two are." She motioned to the television. "It's all over the news."

"Tomorrow," Beau said, tugging Nicky towards the guest room. "We're tired."

"Jake's alive. He's expected to recover," Kailani called after them.

"That's good," Beau said. He looked down at her.

She was happy her boss would make it, but for now, she wanted to push all of that away. To focus on Beau. To enjoy an evening with the first man she'd truly loved.

They barely made it into the bedroom. The moment the door shut, he pushed her up against it and covered her mouth with his as she yanked his shirt open, causing several of his buttons to pop loose and fly all over the room.

He laughed and tugged the skirt to her dress up, running his hands up her legs.

"My god, you have the sexiest legs I've ever had the pleasure of touching." He groaned as he ran his hands up her legs. It felt so good having him touch her. She already ached for him and needed him inside her now.

"Please." She reached for his shorts, but he stepped away. Thankfully, to yank them down and step out of them before returning to press his body against hers.

"I need you now," he said against her skin.

"Yes, please," she repeated.

He had hiked her skirt up and when he ripped her panties away, she laughed and spread her legs wider for him.

"Tell me again," he said as he stepped between her legs. "Tell me as I enter you." His eyes bore into hers.

"I love you," she said as he slipped inside her.

One thing was sure, trying to make wild crazy love quietly in someone's guest room was impossible. When it was over, they could hear the television playing loudly down the hallway.

Nicky chuckled. "Okay, obviously Kailani heard us."

Beau chuckled. "Good, that will pay her back from all the times they've stayed at my place, and I had to turn up the television to drown out her and Matt's groans."

Nicky laughed. "Now I don't feel so bad." She sighed and rested her head on his shoulder. "I love you."

"I love you too." He pulled her closer. "God, I don't think it will ever get old, hearing that from you."

She shifted to look up at him. "You may take that back after meeting my mother. She'll give you the third degree."

He laughed. "Our mothers are going to get along just great."

Nicky's heart was floating as she fell asleep. Her dreams were filled with wonder and joy. Images of her and Beau watching beautiful children, their children, play on the green grass of his yard had her almost flying. She'd always wanted kids, had dreamed of it for a long time. But after James, she'd decided to focus on her career instead.

Everything was so perfect. Until the scream shattered everything.

She felt Beau jump out of bed next to her just as hands gripped her wrist and yanked her from the bed, pulling her upwards. She was shoved and pushed down the hallway and finally thrown on the tile floor of the living room.

She landed right next to Kailani, who was crying and holding her wrist.

Nicky crawled to her and wrapped her arms around the other woman as two men held Beau between them. Each had one of his arms tightly held so that he couldn't move. One of the men had a bloody nose, no doubt thanks to Beau's fist.

Nicky glanced around and noticed that there were four of them. Two held Beau and one stood at the front door, while the other stood over her and Kailani.

The fact that none of them wore masks or tried to hide their identities caused Nicky's stomach to sink. They didn't care if they knew who they were, which meant they didn't plan on leaving anyone that could identify them.

"What do you want?" Nicky asked, although she was pretty sure she already knew the answer.

"Where is your husband?" one man asked Kailani.

"He's... working late," she answered with a cry.

"Oh well, one less body," the man standing by the front door said with a chuckle.

"What do you want?" Nicky asked again.

"From you? Nothing. We were hired to do a job. That's all," the man standing over them said. He lifted his gun towards her chest. "Nothing personal."

A loud growl echoed in the room just before Beau swung his body fully in a circle. Both men holding his arms went flying in different directions. The man who'd been pointing his gun at her turned towards Beau.

In that split second, she thought about losing him. About losing everything she'd just found. Without thinking, she swung up and threw her entire body at him, knocking him and her into the large glass coffee table. She felt the man's body kick under hers as it landed, first on the glass and then again on the floor once the glass shattered under their combined weight.

She had every intention of using all her strength to continue fighting him, to keep him down, only he didn't continue fighting. His body went completely limp under hers.

"Nicky!" Kailani screamed, causing her to jerk her head up. The man who had been guarding the door was rushing towards her. "Here," Kailani pushed the gun, which had just fallen from the unconscious man's hands, towards her. Without thinking, Nicky lifted and fired the gun directly at the man's chest.

It wasn't like she'd seen on the movies. The man instantly dropped. No writhing in pain, no screaming, he just... dropped.

Beau was still fighting one of the two men that had held him, while the other sat dumbfounded on the floor, holding his head as blood flowed from a large gash.

"Stop!" Nicky yelled, holding the gun towards the man. "I'll shoot!" she screamed when he swung out at Beau again. When he still was coming at Beau, she aimed the gun, then at the last minute, yanked it up and shot at the ceiling. The bullet hit the light and shattered the glass, sending shards raining over her as one of the lightbulbs went dark.

Okay, so that wasn't like it happened in the movies either. But it got the job done. The man backed away from Beau and held his hands up as he looked between her and Beau. Then, before she could respond, he turned around and fled out the front door.

Beau made a move as if he was going to chase him, but

then stopped and yanked up the man who was still sitting on the floor, holding his head.

"You're not going anywhere," he told the man, shoving him down on the lounge chair. "Get me some rope," he told Kailani, who nodded and rushed from the room, still holding her wrist.

"Here," Nicky said, handing the gun to Beau. "I think you're better at handling this."

He took the gun from her, not taking his eyes from the man.

"Do you know them?" she asked Beau.

Beau glanced towards the man she'd knocked out and nodded. "That's Joseph. The one that got away was Neil. They work for Glenn on his property," he added. "These two..." He shook his head.

"Here." Kailani came rushing in with several bungie cords. Nicky took them from her. "I think my wrist is broken," she said with a cry. "I... need to call Matt."

"Sit," Beau said calmly. "Call him and the police. Nicky, can you tie him up?"

Kailani was on the phone now, crying and telling Matt to call the police. From what she understood, Matt was already on his way home.

Nicky looked down at the man, who was obviously in shock. "I don't think I have to." She set the bungies down and then walked over to grab a towel from the kitchen counter. The gash on the man's head was worse than she thought it would be. "What'd you hit him with?"

"My fist," Beau answered. "I think he hit his head on the stone there." He motioned to the fireplace.

Nicky pushed the rag against his head and the man looked up at him. "Ma?"

"It's okay, you're going to be okay. Just hold this here," she said easily.

The man nodded and then went back to staring blankly at the windows.

"What about him?" Beau said, motioning to the man she'd knocked out.

Walking over, she shifted the man and then gasped and fell backwards when she noticed his eyes staring straight back at her.

"He's... dead." She closed her eyes for a moment, trying to block out the image of the large piece of glass that had sliced halfway through his neck.

"What about him?" Beau asked, motioning to the man that she'd shot.

"He's dead too," she said, swaying slightly. Then she gasped when Beau fell to his hands and knees.

She rushed over to him and held him in her arms.

"My god," he said with a growl as he buried his hands into her hair. "I thought I was going to lose you."

Tears filled her eyes. "I'm here." She cried and held onto him. "I'm here."

Matt arrived less than five minutes later and instantly recognized the man sitting on the sofa.

"That's Ronny Adams. He's worked for the resort a few times," Matt said as he hugged Kailani.

"Why did he and these other two break in here?" Kailani asked. They could all hear the sirens and knew that any minute the ambulance and the police would be there.

"Glenn," Ronny said as if in a trance. "Paid us to kill anyone who knew."

"Knew what?" Nicky asked, moving over to sit next to the man. He'd lost a lot of blood and was looking extremely pale.

"Paid us to get the treasure. We dove down at night. We've been moving it to his place in Maui. It's all there." He chuckled. "He's going to give us a cut of it too. We'll all have millions." He smiled. "Me, Joe, Neil, and Nick. We've got most of it already. We've been hauling it up for weeks." He laughed again and then slumped forward.

Nicky quickly checked for a pulse and relaxed when she found it. "He's just passed out." She sighed and took the towel and held it firmly against the cut until an EMT rushed in and took over for her.

Kailani was carted out of the house, her wrist placed in a split until it could be x-rayed.

Beau's fists, which he'd bruised, were iced as both the men that she'd killed were wrapped up and hauled away. They told Jay everything that had happened to them.

Beau mentioned that Nicky would be staying at his place to which Jay laughed, "Are you sure you want to stick around this guy? It should be obvious from the past few weeks that he's a lot of trouble."

Nicky laughed. "Technically, I'm the one who caused most of it."

Beau and Nicky stood out on the front porch and watched Glenn Palakiko's place. Row after row of cars were lined up outside. White vans were being loaded with one of the decade's top archeological finds.

They'd watched the news reports from earlier that morning of Glenn being pulled from his condo in Maui in handcuffs. The blonde woman, his current lover, Katrina, followed behind in her own cuffs.

Glenn was shouting over and over at the police, "Do you know who I am?" Katrina just smiled and looked directly into the camera as if this was a photo opp.

When the report came out about the attack at Matt and Kailani's place, Hector immediately recognized that Joseph had been the man that had hired him to steal Nicky's laptop.

Nicky believed that they didn't want any evidence of the treasure. They must have believed that Nicky's team had actually found some and that she had footage of it. Katrina had been assigned to watch Jake closely and destroy any evidence he may have. She'd already wiped Jake's computer of any images of the site. She'd also sent a few emails from his computer to Jake's boss claiming there was nothing to be found. No doubt in hopes that they'd be pulled off the story. If it hadn't been for Jake's persistence, they would have been sent home days after they'd arrived.

Nicky had put more together, estimating that Glenn had teamed up with Jake and her crew to throw them off the trail. His hired goons had even gone as far as to shoot at the boats to scare them away from the site.

They'd all believed that Glenn had been trying to find out the location of the treasure, when in fact, he'd been trying to throw them off the trail instead.

The fact that Glenn had tried to frame Beau for Tomas' murder had thrown him off until Nicky mentioned that if Beau had been locked away for murder, his property would have been free for the taking.

Now, as cars came and went, and camera crews camped on the road just outside his driveway, he knew that it would be a while before things returned to normal.

"I guess things are going to be a little hectic around here for a while," Beau said as he pulled Nicky into his arms. She rested the back of her head against his chest and sighed.

"I like hectic," she said with a chuckle. "I'm going to have to find something to do with myself when this all dies down. I've been thinking of writing a book about our adventures. Maybe a few others I've been on." She shrugged.

"You'd be great at writing." He said with a smile.

"In truth, I don't think I'm going to miss the hectic once things die down though." She added.

He smiled and kissed the top of her head. "Do you know what makes life a little more hectic?" he asked as he turned her around.

"What?" she asked, looking up at him.

"Kids," he answered, searching her eyes.

She smiled and then chuckled. "I like kids."

www.ingramcontent.com/pod-product-compliance
Lightning Source LLC
Chambersburg PA
CBHW030401200726
48286CB00015B/2409